CW01507712

HUNTER

Hunter

SHUANG XUETAO

Translated from the Chinese by
Jeremy Tiang

GRANTA MAGAZINE EDITIONS

Granta Trust, 12 Addison Avenue, London W11 4QR

First published in Great Britain by Granta Magazine Editions, 2025

Copyright © Shuang Xuetao, 2019
English translation copyright © Jeremy Tiang, 2025

Original Chinese edition, 猎人 by 双雪涛, published by
Beijing Imaginist/Beijing Daily Publishing House in 2019.

The moral rights of Shuang Xuetao and Jeremy Tiang
to be identified as the author and translator respectively
of this work have been asserted in accordance with
the Copyright, Designs and Patents Act 1988

'Heart' was first published in the *New Yorker* (October 2023) and
subsequently in *Best Literary Translations 2024* (Deep Vellum, 2024).
'Hunter' was first published in *Granta* 169: China (November 2024).

All rights reserved. This book is copyright material and must not
be copied, reproduced, transferred, distributed, leased, licensed
or publicly performed or used in any way except as specifically
permitted in writing by the publisher, as allowed under the terms
and conditions under which it was purchased or as strictly permitted
by applicable copyright law. Any unauthorised distribution or use of
this text may be a direct infringement of the author's and publisher's
rights, and those responsible may be liable in law accordingly.

A CIP catalogue record for this book is
available from the British Library.

1 3 5 7 9 10 8 6 4 2

ISBN 978 1 73853 624 5(paperback)
ISBN 978 1 73853 625 2 (ebook)

Typeset in Plantin by Patty Rennie

Printed and bound by CPI Group (UK) Ltd, Croydon, CR0 4YY

www.granta.com

The manufacturer's authorised representative in the EU
for product safety is Authorised Rep Compliance Ltd,
71 Lower Baggot Street, Dublin D02 P593
Ireland (arccompliance.com)

MIX
Paper | Supporting
responsible forestry
FSC® C013604

Contents

Heart

BEFORE 2015 I'D NEVER BEEN TO BEIJING, which is quite odd – an adult who's been working a few years ought to have visited the capital for a meeting or a classmate's wedding or simply to view the Chairman's corpse. For some reason, anyway. But I never did – a training session in Shenzhen, a business trip to Sichuan, but never Beijing. I never even got as far as Hebei.

In 2013 I left my job at an advertising firm and started writing fiction. I wrote more than thirty short stories, a few of which were published in the local city journal, which was perpetually on the verge of folding. Then, on 6 November 2015, my ba had a sudden heart attack, the result of a hereditary disease that had already claimed five or six people in my family, the first at the end of the Qing dynasty – my great-great-great-uncle, a superb woodworker who could make anything from a coffin to a comb.

When he was fifty-five his heart exploded and he died on a pile of lumber. It happened so suddenly, leaving him bleeding from every orifice, that his family thought he'd been poisoned. They cut him open and discovered that his heart was full of tiny wood shavings, enough to build a foot-high pagoda.

Ever since then my family has suffered from heart disease, about three in every ten of us, men and women, though it's not as serious now that times have changed – none of us are woodworkers any more, and surgery can save us. The procedure in question involves fitting a tiny engine into one of the heart's chambers to make up for the weakness caused by the organ's abnormal fissures, and placing something like the filter of a water dispenser into the aorta to prevent impurities from entering the heart. This operation wasn't available in my city, L———, at least not anywhere I trusted, mainly because of the difficulty of fitting the filter membrane, which in L——— would be placed by hand, with something like the muscle memory of a carpenter, unlike in Beijing or America, where robots were used. Our health insurance wouldn't be accepted in America, so when my father had his attack I arranged for an ambulance to take us from the local hospital to Beijing.

We were due to set off around seven in the evening. By that time, my father's face was purplish green and he could no longer speak, partly due to the oxygen mask on his face, and he lay on a gurney covered in some sort of blue plastic. A doctor from the ER, a woman of about thirty, slightly plump, with dark brown hair and rimless glasses, would accompany us. She said, I should warn you that it'll take us eight hours to drive there, and it's possible that your father might not make it.

– I understand.

– My name is Xu. I've just graduated – this is my first time on the night ambulance to Beijing, and it's such a serious case I'm a bit worried, so I hope we can work well together.

– Of course.

– When I say work together, what I mean is that you do whatever I say – don't get clever, don't do anything unless I tell you to, don't ask stupid questions.

– Sure, I don't have any questions anyway.

– Are you the only family member coming along?

– Yes, is that okay?

– There really ought to be one more person here. As a doctor I can push the gurney, but if the patient needs to be lifted, one person will have to take his head and another his legs, and I'm not supposed to move him.

– I can handle it myself.

– I need to let you know, no pressure, but there was an incident where the family member dropped the patient and he died. I know you don't want to hear this, but I'm obliged to tell you.

– Understood. You're saying if we don't work well together, my father might fall and die. Cigarette?

– I don't smoke. Have your cigarette and then get on board – hopefully we'll be able to drive through the night without stopping.

As we left the crowded ER some people scurried by, while others sat perfectly still, face in hands. A young woman ran in from the cold wearing pyjamas, blood seeping from a gash between her eyes. A construction worker in a hard hat was helped past us by two of his colleagues. One of his legs was bent to the side like a faucet, and he was hopping along on the other. Outside it was already completely dark. I was halfway through my cigarette when I noticed a cleaner eyeing the smouldering butt, so I stubbed it out and dropped it into his dustpan. As soon as I clambered on board the ambulance, Dr Xu said to the driver, Let's go. We drove past the row of shops selling fruit and funeral goods by the hospital's main entrance, then turned onto the highway. There wasn't much traffic, and the driver kept up a steady pace. He was in green scrubs, with an extra wide collar for his thick neck. All of a sudden it came to me that I should slip him and the doctor a little money. This hadn't occurred to me before, partly because this was such an urgent trip – I'd taken too long deciding whether to go ahead with it – and partly because I'd been spending so much time at home that I wasn't used to being around other people. I scrabbled hopelessly through my rucksack but, as I'd expected, I didn't have much on me. Thinking about the deposit I'd have to put down when we got to Beijing, not to mention all the other expenses I'd need cash for, I felt a wave of despair.

As this was a hereditary disease, every member of my family had their own way of dealing with it: some were always popping pills, some kept getting themselves examined, some just did whatever the hell they wanted and were fine anyway, or fine until they kicked the bucket at around forty or so, usually from alcohol poisoning rather than heart issues. My grandfather's coping mechanism was boxing, a hobby he passed on to his three sons. Of the three, my father, the youngest, showed the least talent – he was born uncoordinated, with a long torso and short legs, unsuited to any sport. He moved slowly, too. Yet he was the one who persisted the longest, continuing to train without a break even when he was sent down to the countryside during the Cultural Revolution, and then after he returned to the city. His trick was to train in secret – very few people outside the family knew that he could box. He woke up early to get in a couple of hours before work every day, and then did another round before bed. I couldn't remember him ever skipping a session. He didn't like talking and wasn't close to anyone. When my grandfather was still around, he'd often say to my father, Hey, No. 3, you keep to yourself too much, that's going to bite you in the ass when you get older. My father never answered him. Then my grandfather died and there was no one left to scold him. That's the virtue of patience.

When I was a kid, I was always pestering my father to teach me a move or two. What do you want to learn? he said. How to hit people so hard they fall right over, I said. I don't know how to do that, he said. Then teach me how not to feel any pain when people hit me, and instead make their hands hurt, I said. I don't know how to do that either, he said. It seems we have very different understandings of what boxing is, I don't think we should talk about it any more. That's how he was, mostly silent, and when he did break his silence to talk about something, he'd be very serious about it. I was only ten at the time, and even so he weighed every word, as if it had to be finely ground, worn down to a flavourless pulp.

Just before my university entrance exam I said to him, You practise boxing three hours a day, and I spend the same amount of time studying, probably more – do you think you're better at boxing than I am at studying?

– Do you think about studying when you're not doing it?

– No way. Work is work and play is play – there has to be a line between them.

– There you go. Even when I'm not boxing, I'm boxing in my heart – not just my heart, my flesh and bones, too. Sometimes I box in my sleep and wake up feeling exhausted, do you know what I mean?

– So how can you prove you're good at boxing?

He thought about it.

– I can't, but let me try a metaphor: let's say a cat falls from the fifth floor and doesn't die. Does the cat have anything to prove?

– How do you know I'm not going to fall from the fifth floor one of these days? If boxing's so great, why not teach me how to do it?

– I can see I'd better not give you any more meta-phors – you can't cope with them. Why should I teach you?

– Because I'm your son.

– What kind of reason is that? Don't think this or that has to happen just because you're my son – I didn't know who you were going to be before you were born.

Losing my temper, I snapped, So go ahead and punch me.

– You think you can get hit whenever you want, just like that? My fists aren't for punching people. Go to bed.

My grandfather was eighty-five when he died in his sleep. One of my uncles died in the violence of the Cultural Revolution; the other was retired and living an unruffled life at home, though I hadn't been in touch with him for a while. In the ambu-lance, my father's foot twitched, and only now did it occur to me that I ought to remove his shoes. His feet were hideously swollen. He lay perfectly still, like a piece of driftwood, his heart rate and blood pressure gleaming on a monitor. Dr Xu looked at his feet and prodded them one at a time with her index finger.

– Is there a problem? I said.

– Why are your father's feet so small?

– What?

– Some people say that the size of your heart is proportional to the size of your feet. That's nonsense, but he really does have tiny feet. And there's something else I don't understand. Judging by my initial examination of your father, his heart really shouldn't still be working. Just look at his stats – they're unimaginable. Heart rate twenty-five, blood pressure eighty over forty. To put it bluntly, he ought to be dead. I haven't been doing this for very long, but even a thirty-year veteran wouldn't have seen many cases like this. What kind of work do you do?

– Me? I don't have a job.

– Why don't you have a job?

– Because I don't want to work, I'm really lazy – is that a kind of illness?

– You don't seem lazy. Lazy people don't usually get so anxious – nothing about you feels lazy to me. If you don't have a job, what do you do?

– Sit around at home.

– What are you, a Buddhist?

– No. Sometimes I get bored and do some typing.

– What kind of typing? Are you an author?

– Yes, fiction. It's childish but I like to write short stories.

– If you're sleepy, go ahead and have a nap. Your father seems stable and I can keep an eye on him.

– That's really dutiful of you. I feel bad.

After a pause, I added, in a small voice, I forgot to get money before we left. I'm sorry about that.

– I'm not dutiful, it's just that I'm new to the job and don't get much say in anything. For the last half year they've stuck me with way too many overnight shifts. I couldn't go to sleep now if I tried, and if I were tired I wouldn't be able to stay awake no matter how much money you gave me. How come an author like you has such strange ideas? Besides, your father has such an unusual condition, anyone working in medicine would want to observe him. Did you say it was hereditary?

– Yes, a hereditary heart disease.

– Who else in your family has it?

– It basically skips a generation. My grandfather was fine, but my great-grandfather died of it.

– Your great-grandfather must have been born around 1900. When did he die?

– I think he was in his twenties, not long after my grandfather was born.

– Was it a Chinese or a western doctor who diagnosed him?

– I don't know, but he definitely died of heart disease.

– How can you be so sure?

– I'm his descendant, of course I know. This is our history.

She didn't respond, and I knew I'd taken the conversation in the wrong direction. I turned to the driver, but all I could see was the back of his neck and his collar. It didn't seem like he'd heard any of our conversation. The ambulance kept going at a steady pace, with almost no braking or sudden turns, yet we'd overtaken a number of speeding vehicles. It was completely dark outside, nothing to see but the looming outlines of the surrounding hills. No honking, no radio. We were flowing through the night like the drip hanging over my father's head, silently infiltrating his unfamiliar veins.

Over the next hour, I began to feel sleepy. If I'd been at home, I'd still have been wide awake – I often stayed up as late as two in the morning even when I had nothing particular to do, flipping through a book or writing a couple of paragraphs or shuffling through music. My father went to bed early and got up early, and never snored, though he did sometimes cough during the night. He was a paint sprayer at a factory and had chronic pharyngitis. He never woke himself up with his coughing. It was part of his sleep, like rolling over. He'd told me that he dreamed about boxing, but I didn't know how true that was – he slept curled up, hugging his shoulders, taking up as little space as possible, as if the bed were full of other people hemming him in. In the summer, his blanket ended up between his legs, and he always wore a yellowing singlet rather than going shirtless. In the winter, he had the covers pulled up to his neck, but even then I could see from the outline of his body that he was in the same shrunken posture.

I drifted off for what must have been ten minutes or so before jolting awake, assaulted by guilt – what if he'd died in those ten minutes? This brief nap seemed to have lasted years, as if I'd been out so long the entire world had transformed. Dr Xu was studying my father's hands, first from where she was sitting, opposite me, and then moving closer and squatting next to him. What's wrong? I said. Does your father play the piano? she said. No, he's a labourer, I said. Look, his fingers are moving, she said. I knelt by the gurney. His left hand was anchored in place by the drip tube and remained motionless. On his right index finger was a clip connected to the display screen, and as I watched he pushed the clip off with his thumb, then all five fingers thrummed on the edge of the mattress, over and over, never pausing in their tap-tapping, from his little finger to his thumb, maybe a dozen times before he tried unsuccessfully to replace the clip.

Dr Xu glanced at the monitor.

– His heart rate is still falling at the same speed. What's going on?

– I don't know.

She waited a moment, made sure his hand wasn't going to start moving again, put the clip back on, and sat back down, still mumbling *What's going on?* to herself.

– My father's boxed ever since he was a kid.

– What kind of boxing?

– No idea, but it's always the same style of boxing. He'll practise for a few hours at a time, always the same moves, once in the morning and once at night.

– In a park?

– No, in his bedroom.

– Martial arts in a bedroom?

– Yes, summer and winter alike.

– Right, so this must be a nerve spasm or muscle memory. It's not uncommon. Remember, your father is dying, his heart is weakening, and I'm not sure we'll make it to Beijing.

– But his fingers were moving so steadily.

– That doesn't matter. Sometimes our bodies do that as camouflage – you should prepare yourself.

– If it happens like you say, what should we do?

– Drive straight back. He's probably no longer in pain. How should I put this? It's like a balloon slowly deflating, that's about the same thing.

– That comparison causes me pain.

– Your pain and his pain are two different things.

– Yes, though you can't do anything about either.

I regretted the words as soon as they were out of my mouth, because why should I expect her to be able to do anything? She was only an emergency-room doctor, a stranger who was in this vehicle for god knows what reason. I apologize, I said, that's not your responsibility. She reached out to lift my father's blanket and said, No need to apologize, everything you said is true. Give me a hand, he needs a new pee pad.

We drove on a while longer. I glanced out the window and noticed that the traffic was growing sparser. We'd probably crossed into Hebei province, and it must have been roughly three in the morning. For the past hour, I'd been pondering my father's funeral. They were a real headache, the countless tasks that lay ahead: contacting relatives I hadn't spoken to in ages, getting their phone numbers from a palm-sized book my father kept by his bedside. He'd retired from a state-run factory only to get another job spraying paint for a private firm, which he'd done right up until he fell ill, and so I probably ought to reach out to his co-workers; they'd usually be the ones to chip in for his funeral expenses and send a few vehicles for the procession. I imagined myself sitting in an office in that struggling little factory, discussing these things with some indifferent middle-aged man, feeling even more stressed than I was now. All of this I would have to navigate on my own, whereas on this night I at least had two other people with me, and my father could take on his share of the responsibility, because no matter what condition he was in he was still participating in my life and, burdensome as this was, when he died there would only be me left in my life, totally alone. I guess that's what freedom looks like nowadays, but when that happened, would I still need to write? My father had never expressed any opinions about my writing – in fact, he hadn't read a single word of my stories – but even so, had I been writing for his sake? If not, why was I so doubtful now?

I told myself that of course I had to keep writing – I wasn't doing it for him, he didn't know anything, I was writing for everyone in the world except him

– but these conclusions just rattled around inside my head, like echoes from someone shouting into a deserted valley.

Around three-thirty in the morning, Dr Xu said, I'm starting to feel a bit sleepy. Shut your eyes for a while then, I said. I'll nap for half an hour, she said. Keep an eye on the drip and his heart rate, and wake me if anything seems irregular. All right, I said. She lay down on her seat, using her arm as a pillow, and dropped off straight away, her head and feet pointing in the same direction as my father's. Four o'clock came and she slept on, but I didn't wake her because my father's vitals showed no sign of changing; they weren't plummeting as she'd predicted. I didn't feel tired at all, though my ass hurt from sitting still for so long and I had to wiggle it around. Then all of a sudden I needed to pee; the urge came out of nowhere, like someone pulling a sink plug. I said to the driver in a low voice, Hey, I need to pee, is there a rest area coming up? He didn't answer and kept facing the road. I didn't think I could hold it in much longer, so I scuttled to the front and said, Sir, sorry to bother you, but I need to use the bathroom. Still he said nothing, as if he found my request so ridiculous that merely replying would wound his dignity. I tapped his shoulder and said, Sir, I'm about to piss myself, could you stop? That's when I looked in the rearview mirror and saw that his eyes were shut. Startled, I thought, Wait, I must be mistaken – does he just have small eyes? I leaned forward and, no, he was fast asleep, breathing evenly, in through the nose and out through the mouth, even snoring lightly, every muscle in his face relaxed, a faint sheen of grease shining in the streetlights, his hands still on the wheel. There was a slight bend in the road up ahead, and without hesitation he guided the vehicle around it, stepping on the accelerator and the clutch as needed. I grabbed his shoulder and shook him, but he didn't wake up. Next I pinched the back of his neck, but again, nothing. He just jolted as if a needle had pierced his bum, rising a little from his seat before settling back down. We were going about ninety miles per hour, and I couldn't stir him.

My bladder felt like an unruly schoolchild waiting for the final bell. I walked back to my father's side, lifted his blanket, and pulled the pee pad out from under him. It was still perfectly dry, just a bit warm. I glanced at Dr Xu, but she was sound asleep, so I pulled down my trousers and let rip. The liquid was quickly absorbed, even though I had so much to let out that by the time I was done the pad looked like a cotton-stuffed quilt and was much heavier than

before. I stuffed it back under my father, his withered legs with a red birthmark on the right thigh.
I'd known this was there when I was a kid, but I'd
forgotten about it till now. After tucking myself back
into my trousers, I tapped Dr Xu and said, Hey, wake
up! The driver's asleep, we need to do something.
She didn't move so I grabbed her arm and pulled it
out from under her head. She fell from her seat, but
remained asleep. I checked her breathing. She was
still alive, only her face looked more anxious than
before; her brow was furrowed, and she let out occasional sighs, her head bumping against the floor of
the ambulance. I bundled her back onto the bench
and she suddenly asked, How much longer? I don't
know, I said. Give me a bit more time, I'm almost
done, she said. Then silence.

I sat back down. There were no other vehicles in
sight, just the rising night fog, a sort of milky white
haze in all directions. We must have been approaching Beijing. Now I realized that as well as forgetting
to get cash I'd also neglected to bring any reading
material. At this point I desperately needed a book
to whisk me away from this place. Even an out-of-
date literary journal would have done the job. I tried
hard to remember something I'd read recently. A
poem popped into my mind, or rather half a poem;

I couldn't remember the poet, but a writer friend had posted it online:

> Still young, still idealistic, leftist too but wearing
> A rightist's hat. He starved himself plump in
>   Xinjiang,
> Fled back home to Changsha. Grandma made him
> Pork-tripe radish soup, red dates floating in it.
> Incense burning indoors, a rising perplexity.
> On this day, he has no idea what to do.

There was more, but I'd forgotten it. Grandma and soup. Nourishing images, which was probably why it had come to me; I needed comforting thoughts at this moment to show me that human connection actually existed in this world, something that gave off heat, a scene with a little noise and bustle, anything to dispel my current sinking perplexity. Dr Xu's face knocked against the back of the seat from time to time, until I rested my rucksack under it, nice and soft since all I'd brought was a jacket and two packets of tissues. The driver continued expertly piloting the vehicle, and I could only assume that he was keeping tabs on the road ahead and the rear-view mirror with his ears.

★

Once, when I was little, my father and I spoke about death. I'd asked, Today Big Fatty said he was going to beat me to death – can he do that? If he wants to he can, said my father. He was rinsing vegetables at the time – he could cook a few simple dishes, but refused to touch potatoes or radishes, because when he got sent down to the countryside that was all he had to eat and they wrecked his stomach. Nowadays when he saw them at the vegetable market he'd walk quickly by.

– Then what happens after I'm dead? Can I get revenge?

– No, you'd be completely defeated.

– Are you going to die?

– Yes, I might die at any moment. The human body has a heart in it, about the size of your fist, and when it stops beating you die.

– Why would it stop? It's beating now, it will beat tomorrow – why would it stop one day?

– It's beating now, but it might not tomorrow. Though your heart is very healthy. You aren't going to die because of that.

– How would you know?

– I listened to it when you were born. I heard your heart and it's a healthy one. Besides, my heart has problems, so the probability is that yours doesn't

– those are reasonable odds. Anyway, let's leave it at that. The next time Big Fatty wants to hit you, you should run away as fast as you can, then you won't die.

Dr Xu rolled over, but nimbly avoided falling off the bench. I shut my eyes too. Now everyone in the ambulance had their eyes shut, and we entered a common darkness. All of a sudden I heard coughing. First I thought it must be the driver, but I quickly realized that it sounded too familiar to be him, like someone crumpling sandpaper. I opened my eyes to see my father hacking away, more and more violently. Finally, he woke himself up. Ba, I said. He looked at me and sat up. As always, now that he was awake, the coughing stopped.

– What's all this?

– We're almost in Beijing.

– Beijing? What for?

– To get you treatment, you had a heart attack.

– Forget it. I saw my own heart a moment ago, it's been gnawed at by worms, it's all rusty now. A worm had a chat with me, it said it knew my grandfather. Are you going to Beijing too?

– Yes, who else would take care of you?

– What nonsense, I don't need to be taken care of. What's the time?

– Five-twenty in the morning.

– I haven't boxed yet today. Help me get rid of this pee pad, it smells revolting.

With that, he crawled out from under the blanket and stood there, boxing. After twenty minutes, he sat down.

– I've forgotten what comes next.

– How's that possible? You've been practising this sequence for forty years.

– It's gone, I don't remember a single bit of it. My whole life has gone past, just like that.

– It's not over yet, you're doing perfectly well now, aren't you?

– My whole life has gone past. I always knew it would, I knew my life would slip by, that's why I took up boxing, because what else could I do? And now I've forgotten the boxing too. I feel light. I've finally gotten through it, I've spent it all.

– Would you like some water?

– I'm not thirsty. What are your plans?

– I don't know. I'm still not able to accept a life that doesn't have you in it. Please hold on a while longer.

– You think too highly of my existence. The probability is that your life has more meaning, your existence devours mine. From the day you were born you've been eating my existence bit by bit with a little spoon, but that doesn't matter, you don't need to feel guilty. When do you plan to get married?

– I haven't given it any thought.

– Mm, well, when you have a son, you'll eat him with a spoon too, that's how good your appetite is. Like I said, I listened to your heart when you weren't looking – it's sturdy as an airplane engine. You can't hear it, but I can – it roars by my side every single day. That's why I'm quiet.

And then he actually did fall silent for a while, the way he often did, stopping in the middle of a conversation. Who knows what he was thinking? Maybe he'd just forgotten what he was about to say. Dr Xu rolled over again, this time with her face towards us. Her eyes were open, but I wasn't sure if she could see us. What you're saying isn't any help to me, she said with absolute certainty, no help at all. There's nothing else I can do – it's perfectly clear in the images, and every instrument tells me the truth, so there's no point to your lying. History doesn't lie. History has proved that people like you are no help. Give me your medical records. She rapped lightly at her head, eyes half shut. Who wrote this? What kind of handwriting is this? No one could read it!

My father didn't respond. His face was full of incomprehension. He had no idea what she was getting at, or why there would be such a patient in the ambulance. Her entire body juddered, as if someone had kicked her, and her eyes drifted shut again.

Give me a hand, said my father, I'm heading back. As I lifted him onto the gurney he wrapped his arms around me. He didn't stink, but rather had the light, pleasant scent of a small child. Into my ear he said, Goodbye, this is as far as we'll go. No, I said, don't say that, you're not old yet. You have to wait till you're an old man. Goodbye, he said again. As his eyes lost focus, I said, Don't fall asleep, we're almost there. His eyes widened a little and he said, Who are you? I'm your son, I said. He nodded and said, Safe travels, take care. With that he lay flat, reaching out to cover himself with the blanket. He fell asleep, coughed a couple of times, and stopped breathing.

The monitor began beeping, waking Dr Xu. She groped around, realized there was nothing next to her, then woke fully. She asked who'd put a rucksack under her head, and when I said I had, she said it was very uncomfortable. I told her two things had happened: the driver had been fast asleep for quite a while, and my father had died. I could tell she wanted to comfort me, but her professionalism held her back. She nodded and removed his drip as if she were unravelling a sweater back into yarn. After a few minutes the driver woke too, looking unabashed, but then nothing bad had happened, so fair enough. Besides, the nap had left him refreshed, as if his day were just beginning. He turned and spoke to Dr Xu, and they decided we should go back the way we came. I asked Dr Xu if we could stop so I could go to the bathroom, and we did at the next rest area. When I got back, I made sure the other two were still awake, then I curled up next to my father's legs. I felt light, free of burdens, free of goals, and to the accompaniment of my own heartbeat I soon fell asleep.

Yang Guangyi

I THINK IT MUST HAVE BEEN CLOSE TO THE END of 1996 when a wave of unrest came over the factory. Not unrest as in an uprising, this was mostly in people's hearts. No one knew how it started, but it passed from one person to the next until finally even I, a thirteen-year-old child, was aware of it.

The story was that Yang Guangyi had been stabbed. I heard this from my neighbour Zhao Jing, another factory brat a year older than me. Her ma was a bookkeeper in workroom five, and her ba a cadre in the security department. They'd heard about the stabbing through different channels and compared notes at the dinner table. Knowing I was obsessed with Yang Guangyi, Zhao Jing told me. She figured the information had to be accurate. Obviously I didn't believe her. It was the weekend, and Zhao Jing came specially to the workroom where we lived to tell me. I remember she was wearing a yellow sweater, and her keys were hanging from a string around her neck. She told me what she knew down to the last detail – not that she knew many details, she was just repeating her parents' conversation.

Hey, Qin, her ba had said. It seems that Yang Guangyi . . . Yes, said her ma, I heard something happened. Tell me, he said. Seems Yang Guangyi got into a knife fight and was stabbed in the thigh. That's not right, he said, it wasn't a knife fight, it was a sneak attack. Yang Guangyi was walking down the east end of Yanfen Street when he stopped at Old Dou's for an ice pop. He had the popsicle in his mouth and was reaching into his pocket to pay when someone came over, stuck a knife in his bum, and ran off again. Did Old Dou tell you that? she said. I heard it from Dou Peng in workroom three, he said. He came over at lunch for a game of poker. How much did you lose? she asked. Nothing. I broke even, he replied. Won a few rounds to start with actually. Dou Peng's a dirty stop-out, can you trust him? she said. How much *did* you lose? To be honest, I won five yuan but I spent it on a pack of Red Pagodas, he said. After this the conversation turned away from Yang Guangyi.

I didn't entirely believe any of this, but I had to acknowledge it was possible. After school I'd gone to the factory bathhouse and people were talking about it there, too – though it was just shreds and whispers, nothing concrete. There were differences in the shape of the rumours, but the core was the same: a few days ago, who knows where or why, Yang Guangyi had been stabbed.

Yang Guangyi had once been a worker at the factory, but that was a decade ago. He'd stopped showing up after he became a bladesman. After that he was nowhere to be found. His parents came to the factory looking for him, and so did his big sister. He'd gotten married in town and his wife, a strapping country woman, showed up with their daughter in tow, but they were all wasting their time. His wife told the bosses that he'd set off in the summer of 1982 to help a farmer fix a tractor from their factory. After-sales service was brand new back then, and though Yang Guangyi was a little too fond of doing things his own way, his skills weren't bad and he thought of himself as a bit of an inventor, so the workroom dispatched him. He spent three weeks away and returned much thinner. After getting home he gobbled down three bowls of rice, drank a full kettle of water, then produced a short knife from his jacket. His wife said it was curved, maybe a handspan long and double-edged. It had a wooden handle with animals carved into it. Yang Guangyi sat there staring at the knife for a very long time, then he said, Hey honey, I've learned some knife skills. He tucked the knife back into his jacket and went to sleep fully dressed. The next morning, she woke up to find he'd vanished with all his stuff. It was as if he'd never been there. This was the only eye-witness account that connected Yang Guangyi with knives, but in the ten years since, the association had become an article of faith, and no rumour was allowed to contradict it.

Yang Guangyi was never seen in these parts after that. Factory management and the Yang family remained suspicious of one another, each assuming the other had concealed Yang for some nefarious reason, though neither could say what on earth that reason might be. Ten days later, an old poplar tree at the Yanfen Street junction behind the factory, seven or eight metres tall and over sixty centimetres in diameter, was cleaved in two – split down the middle. The two halves remained joined at the root, but you could see daylight through them. A crowd gathered, trying to understand what had happened. If the tree had been struck by lightning, wouldn't it have been scorched? But the poplar leaves were still jade green and flourishing, and the tree clearly wasn't dead (I picked up a bit of botanical know-ledge later, learning that trees receive nutrients through their bark). Anyway, it hadn't rained the night before. Fifteen days later, someone flung five dead sparrows at the factory gate. These were also split down the middle, so that each part only had one eye and one wing, perfect mirror images. The cut was so neat you could tell right away it had been done in a single blow.

There was a guy at the factory who studied martial arts, his name was Chen Pi, as in 'leather', which of course was a nickname – his real name was Chen Ping, but nobody called him that. He was a mechanic, an honest guy who never used his fighting skills to bully anyone, though when he got angry he'd bang his fist down on a wooden table and sometimes snap off the corner. He brought the five sparrows into the workroom and studied them for a long time. They weren't the result of a scientific experiment, he told everyone. Someone had caught the birds by surprise and sliced them in two. He'd heard of people in ancient times with godlike blade skills, people who could cut a tiger in half but also finely slice a leaf. They used a blade not much longer than the human head called a hand-knife, one that grew out of the hand as if the whole arm was a sword. When the blade left the hand it became a flying dagger. The last of these bladesmen, said Chen Pi, is Yang Guangyi.

Now everyone understood the connection, and said with sudden enlightenment, Oh, Yang Guangyi, it was Yang Guangyi. But what was he trying to do? Never mind what he wants to do, Chen Pi said. I have a small house on Ninth Street, fifty-odd ping in area, I'll give it to him and become his disciple. Anyone who sees him please let him know.

The factory manager called Chen Pi into his office, so Chen Pi went in.

– You were looking for me?

– Why the hell are you eating shit?

– I'm not eating shit.

– Then why is shit coming out of your mouth? I clearly told you that the police and factory security had a joint meeting yesterday and decided that even though Yang Guangyi hasn't done anything, he still needs to be arrested. Why are you going on about godlike blades? The man's one of the dregs of society. He's openly challenging public order. Get a message to him: as long as there's a single person left in this place, we'll capture him. We treated him like talent to start with, and now look, a couple of weeks away and he's turned into a martial arts

vagrant. We're not trying to punish him – we're trying to rescue him. You understand?

– I don't know Yang Guangyi.

– I don't care whether you know him or not,
aren't you his disciple? You're involved now. You're
part of our militia. From now on you won't be going
home at night, we'll find you somewhere else to stay
so that you can patrol the factory.

Chen Pi thought about this for a long time. Then
you'll have to give me a cattle prod and a hard hat,
he said. The hard hat is the crucial thing.

The reason I know all this is because Chen Pi
was my father. Back then, before I was born, he was
wildly ambitious. But a few years later he was fat and
the little kung fu he knew went fallow, quite possibly
as a result of that conversation with management.
He spent the next couple of months wandering the
factory in a hard hat, to no avail. After the tree and
the sparrows, Yang Guangyi never demonstrated his
skills again. So my father patched up the fifty-ping
house, got married and moved in. That was at the
start of 1983, before I existed – I was born that
winter. Not long after, when I was less than a month
old, Yang Guangyi showed himself again.

In the early summer of 1983 there had been a
spate of arson attacks in the city: within three months

a grain administration bureau, a boiler house, two homes (both on Yanfen Street), a textile warehouse and a police car parked by the side of the road had all been set alight. Two people died: a former soldier who'd been walking past the boiler house when it went up and charged in to save whoever he could, and a six-year-old girl who'd dozed off while hiding from her family in a cupboard as a prank. The squad car was the strangest case of all. It belonged to an officer who'd been investigating the string of fires; he'd parked it across the road from an auto repair shop and had got out to ask questions. A few minutes later the car was ablaze, and before long it was reduced to a metal frame.

After this the nature of the case fundamentally changed. Was someone trying to incite a rebellion? For a while the whole city was on the lookout for the culprit. The police put a notice in the papers, short and to the point because they could only be certain of one thing: the arsonist had to know kung fu. Not that he was flying over rooftops or running up walls – but he was definitely light on his feet. The officer whose car was burned said that although he hadn't been able to make out any details in the dark, he'd spotted someone fleeing the scene. In less than five seconds the figure had climbed a tree with a couple of bounds, then jumped over a wall. Two months of vigilance produced nothing, not a single arrest. There was no link between the fires, which probably meant they were just someone's hobby and not meant to kill anyone. They did stop, though, and then it was as if nothing had happened.

My ba told me later that the police came to the factory several times looking for Yang Guangyi, and that the directors got hauled to the station repeatedly for questioning, all with the intent of tracking down Yang, whom they simply couldn't find. My ba was interrogated for a whole afternoon. The first thing they asked him was why he'd wanted to be Yang's disciple. I guess I was paying the price for having a dream, he told me. It felt like a noble thing to say at the time, but now it was a stain on my life. He swore up and down that he never knew Yang Guangyi personally. They'd been in different workrooms, and the factory employed over ten thousand workers. They'd never spoken to each other, never even crossed paths, and the only reason my ba knew any martial arts was because my grandfather had taught him some as a form of strength training. He'd never actually been in a fight. The most he could do was chop off a table corner, and that only took an explosive burst of energy. The police then asked him to bring out the five sparrows, but my ba said the sparrows were killed more than a year ago so of course they'd long since been thrown away – it's not like they were such remarkable specimens that they deserved to be preserved in formaldehyde. That riposte earned him two days in the lockup. Before letting him out, they made him sign a statement. He wrote: I don't know Yang Guangyi. If he's the arsonist then I cannot support him, and if I am destined to ever meet him, I will detain him no matter the cost. That said, Yang Guangyi is trained in the blade, not in running away, and I urge our policeman comrades to consider other suspects. Even in his sixties, my ba still remembered these words. I only cared about the truth, he told me. These days, I'd keep my mouth shut. When I was young, though, words tumbled out without going through my brain.

Early in the morning five days later, around the time the loudspeakers began playing 'The East is Red', the night watchman Old Ma noticed a sack when he was opening the factory gates. It was too heavy to move. Had burglars robbed the factory and left the bag behind in their haste to get away? Old Ma looked inside, screamed and went into shock. His mouth would stay twisted to one side for more than a decade. Inside the sack was a man's body, chopped in two, along with a pair of white gloves and a plastic container of gasoline. The cops arrived, glanced at the contents of the bag, and took it away. The victim was an unemployed twenty-one-year-old who'd failed the university entrance exam three years in a row. Some said he'd flunked the political check, while others said his nerves had made him mess up the papers all three times. He'd never trained in martial arts, but he did have extraordinarily long limbs. Not much to speak of above the belly button, all leg below. One hundred and seventy-five centimetres and only ninety jin. He'd been cut in half so neatly that even his eyebrows were perfectly intact. Each half weighed exactly forty-five jin. The arson case was solved just in time for a murder investigation to begin.

This time, there was no denying that the crime was the work of Yang Guangyi. Obviously it wouldn't be easy to catch him. Half a year later, there'd still been no progress. We heard he'd been fired on at Twelfth Line vegetable market, but managed to get away. Someone wrote an op-ed that aroused a lot of discussion, asking whether we should be treating Yang Guangyi as a hero instead. Nothing came of that – debates and catching criminals are two different things, and don't affect each other. Not that they caught him. Perhaps Yang Guangyi was a hero, because if the arsonist hadn't been caught everyone's safety and possessions would have stayed at risk. Still, his tactics seemed crueller than necessary, so it was hoped that Mr Yang would surrender to the authorities. The general consensus was that a balance had to be found between justice and humanity. Within the next month, more than ten people turned themselves in: some were men named Yang, others martial artists skilled with the blade. All were released after a round of persuasive education, and the matter was considered closed.

Not entirely closed, though. My ba was still entangled – though not the same kind of entanglement as before, this was a new variety. People kept showing up at our home, not just from our city but from all over, bearing gifts and money. Are you Yang Guangyi's disciple? they would ask. My ba would answer, No, I'm a mechanic. Then the visitors would say, You're being so modest, Master Chen. Here's a small token of my esteem, I hope you'll pass it on to Grandmaster Yang. Please ask him to take care of himself and, if possible, put in a good word for me: Lin Haifei from Hubei. Please take this away, my ba would say. I'm not going to see him. But the visitor would insist on leaving the gift. Master Chen, one said, I've lost my job because our director ran our factory into the ground. He has a mistress whom he wastes all our money on – could you please say something to Grandmaster Yang and have him killed? Go stage a sit-in in the middle of the road, my ba said. It's no use coming to me, I don't know Yang Guangyi. The visitor wrote the director's name and address on a piece of paper and stuck it into the doorframe as he left. Then there was the guy who showed up with an infantry sword and said, Let's have a round of swordplay. I don't know kung fu, said my ba. Then ask Yang Guangyi to show himself, the guy retorted. I don't know where to find him. Why can't you people get that into your heads? Now please put away your crappy sword. C'mon, just one round, said the guy. Let me see what you're made of. Okay, enough is enough, said my ba, I'm calling the police.

My ma later told me that during this time my ba kept shouting in his sleep, the same two lines over and over. One was: I'm not him, are you all deaf? I'm not a black cat and I'm not a white cat, I'm a dog. The other was: Yang Guangyi you motherfucker.

So there we were, the key around Zhao Jing's neck going clink clink clink because she was jumping as she spoke. It was as if the words sloshing out of her were water, and could only be produced through motion.

– That's not possible.

– Why not?

– Yang Guangyi couldn't possibly have been stabbed, not in a sneak attack and not in a fight.

– He did so get stabbed, everyone in the factory knows – just admit it.

– Oh, so I have to believe it just because everyone else does? Yang Guangyi's the very best. He's the one who wounds others, he never gets wounded himself.

– That's what I used to think, but my teacher says that all skills take constant practice to keep up. Maybe he hasn't been practising for all these years. Then he wouldn't be as good as he used to be. And arrogance just makes people get worse.

– Why's he been hiding away all these years then? If he was arrogant, he'd have revealed himself long ago. I bet he practises every day, and he hasn't got worse at all, in fact I bet he's gotten even better.

– Why don't you ask your ba?

– How many times have I told you, my ba doesn't know him! I see my ba every day. You think he's lying to me?

– What if he's just pretending? Haven't you seen

39

No Regrets? That tall, skinny guy stayed undercover for so many years.

– Is he my father or yours? Why don't you go home and do your homework? Worry about your problems and not mine.

She kept pestering me for a while longer before leaving. Her ba was off to play cards that night, and she was afraid she'd get back and find him arguing with her ma.

I eyed my parents over dinner. Surely they knew what had happened, but neither of them said anything. I didn't either. After we ate they got ready to see my grandfather. He'd had a stroke and now they visited him every weekend. The fifty-ping house had been demolished by then, which is why we had come to live in the factory compound. The house had actually been under my grandfather's name, though he and my grandmother were now living with my aunt and her husband, who took care of them. That's why my parents felt obligated to stop by, to say: we haven't forgotten the old folk, and you shouldn't forget us either – let's all remember each other.

It snowed that night, lightly at first, then with increasing force. The wind rose into a howl against the workroom windows. You might as well stay behind, my ma said. I can't be bothered to carry you through all that. I want to see Yeye, I said. He only recognizes three people, and they're all his children, she said. There's not even any point me going, so why would you want to go? He recognized me last time, I said. No, she said, he thought you were your ba as a child. Just stay here, and if we get back early I'll buy you two squares of rice cake from Qiulin. My ba said nothing, he just did the dishes, got dressed and left with my ma. I watched from the second-storey window as they wheeled their bicycles into the snow, wobbling against the wind. Finally they managed to get moving, and though it seemed they weren't making any progress, they eventually passed through the factory gates and disappeared into the blizzard.

It's started snowing less since then – as little as one brief storm over an entire winter, I've heard, and very sparse snow at that, barely covering the tyres of cars before diminishing into rain. Whenever my ma phones these days, she complains that it hasn't snowed yet, and everything looks dull to her and my ba. The blizzard I remember best was in the winter of '96, I told her on one of these calls. I was home alone, and I was so frightened that the two of you wouldn't come back.

– That's nonsense, when did we ever leave you home alone?

– There was that one time you and Ba went to see Yeye. Around the time we heard that Yang Guangyi had been stabbed.

– We never did that. Your grandfather loved you most of all. If we'd shown up without you, he'd have beaten your ba with his stick.

– Yeye didn't know me by then.

– Even after he'd forgotten everyone else, he recognized you as soon as you stepped in the door. Your auntie used to complain that they were the ones cleaning up his piss and shit, but it was this little bastard of a grandson who got all the love.

– I guess that's possible. Maybe I'm remembering it wrong.

– You're not remembering it wrong. You've completely forgotten all of it.

Around ten-thirty that night, I woke up and glanced at my electronic watch. I sensed I wasn't alone in the building. The space was cavernous. We'd been there a year at that point, and I'd trained myself to spring awake whenever someone came in at night. Pulling on a hoodie, I went to the second-storey window and looked down. The snow had stopped, and moonlight was pouring over the pathway through the compound, an endless silver river. The intruder's footsteps weren't particularly light, and I could hear him clearly as he came up to the second floor. Rummaging in my stationery box I found a craft knife, and I pushed the blade out with my thumb as far as it would go. My parents and I slept in separate storerooms – theirs was slightly larger and had bunk beds made of wooden boards. Their door would be ajar, because they were still out. My room was about ten metres away from theirs, on the same side of the corridor. The intruder stopped outside their room, probably pausing to pull the door all the way open. Next, I heard him walk over to my door. After about five seconds, I heard a voice say, Is anyone there? I didn't reply. Is Chen Pi there? No, I said. Ah, are you Chen Pi's son? he asked. Who are you? I said. My name is Yang Guangyi, he said. Surname Yang, Guangyi as in 'broad meaning', as in the opposite of 'narrow meaning'.

I opened the door and saw a young man standing there, maybe twenty-seven or twenty-eight, broad shoulders, square face, no hat, short hair, grey padded jacket, neat and tidy, holding a pair of black leather gloves. You're lying, I said. You're too young. You'd have to call Yang Guangyi 'uncle'. Where's your ba? he said. He and my ma went to see my yeye, I said. He knows the real Yang Guangyi, now get out of here, he'll be home soon. Oh, he said. I heard he wanted to study kung fu with me? That was a long time ago, I said. I've only just heard, he said. Information takes a while to reach me. Hey, do you have anything to eat? I thought about it. No, just an apple. Let's split it, he said. Give me the smaller half, I'm a bit thirsty. I rubbed the apple on my trouser leg and cut it in two with the craft knife. He took his half and said, Neatly sliced. He devoured it in three bites. Got a cigarette? No, I said. I've given you an inch and now you want a mile. He laughed. That's true, well said.

All of a sudden I noticed he was moving unsteadily, putting all his weight on his right leg. My heart beat faster. I felt hot blood and the dreams of many years rushing through my head. Did you really get stabbed? I asked. Yes, he said, pointing at the spot. In the back of my thigh – not with a knife, it was an awl. Went a whole inch in. Who did it? I asked. I didn't get a good look at him, he said. Didn't turn around. Why not? I said. I was afraid that if I turned around, I'd have to kill the guy. Then he laughed, and I learned something that no one else knew: Yang Guangyi was a person who liked to laugh, though his laughter came when you least expected it.

It hasn't been easy for your ba all these years, he said, but it hasn't been easy for me either. We've each had our difficulties. Show me your hand. I stretched out my arm so he could prod at my fingers and press on my shoulders. Okay, you'll do, he said. I don't have much time, I can't wait for your ba, but I'll teach you some blade skills so this won't be a wasted trip. With that he produced a curved knife from his jacket, smaller than I'd imagined, only slightly longer than a hand. With a twist he pulled it into two blades. You have two knives? I said. Yes, he said, this is a double blade. The left one is called Narrow, the right is Broad. Together they're the Narrowbroad Knives. This won't be difficult, I'll just explain it to you and you'll get it right away. I don't really need both knives, so I'll leave you one.

I didn't take the knife he held out to me. On his face was a smile of pure innocence. I don't want to learn, I said. You don't? No, I said. Why not? I have school tomorrow, I said, and I'm on classroom duty so I should get to bed. Do you know how many peo- ple . . . he started to say. I know, I said, but I don't want to learn. Also, I was lying earlier, I have another apple – here, take it with you. I took the apple from where it sat next to my pillow and placed it in his hand. He accepted it, a little distracted, and nodded

45

after a moment. Tucking away the knives, he said, I guess I got carried away. You're just a kid, you don't understand yet. Tomorrow at school I'll have to mop the floor, I said, then I'll have to hand out the self-study assignments to all my classmates. Fine, he said, that's that then, are we quits? Yes, I said. And I'm not going to tell my ba. I trust you, he said. You ever want to see me again, just place an apple under the paw of the stone lion at Beiling Park's east gate. We can have a chat. I'll remember that, I said. He smiled at me, turned and left. I watched from the window, but didn't see him emerge.

I've eaten quite a few apples in the years since. To be honest, they're my favourite fruit, and I've never wasted a single one.

Up at Night

YUE XIAOQI PHONES ME AROUND NINE BUT I'M
still playing soccer at Si'de Park and I miss his call.
By the time I've changed and can call him back,
he's not answering. I get home and have a shower
while Ge'er makes dinner. Our earnings have been
down recently so we let our helper go. One of the
stunt doubles on the film I was shooting died, and
that affected morale so badly that we had to stop
production. Ge'er's been struggling with her novel,
which has sent her into a tailspin. Just the fact that
she made dinner tonight probably means she's hit
a good stretch. A few days ago she announced she
was skipping dinner because eating sent blood to
her brain, which prevented her from working. She
wouldn't let me eat either. According to her I look
overly contented after I've had my dinner, and that
annoys her. Hunger keeps me looking humble.
When she was starting on this novel I said to her,

47

Maybe you should wait. Now that you're pregnant your office might not let you take on such a big project. She said it wasn't her decision, a voice was telling her what to write, and she could grow a baby at the same time. For the past two months she's been running around doing research with a private eye named Huang. He used to work at a legal firm until he offended one of the higher-ups and got tossed into prison for a few months. A few days after his release, they accused him of soliciting prostitutes and locked him up for another fortnight. When he got out, he resigned and struck out on his own. I ask Ge'er if he'd actually been with a hooker and she says well not exactly, the woman came to him for help with a court case. What case? I ask. One of her clients smeared a chemical substance on his condom and now she can never have children, she says. Good god, I say. It wasn't his first time either, she says. He did the same thing in Shanghai and Wuhan. He's a retired college professor. Used to research reproduction. How did the woman track him down? I say. He'd hired her before, she says. Got it, I say. But why are you writing about all this? You're a producer, not an author, she says. Don't ask questions outside your area of expertise. Remember our motto: you're the man of the world, I'm the artist. Right, I say, but the child's mine too, and my work as a father began the night I met you. I'm stuck at home all day, she says, and I always feel like drinking. Do you think alcohol would hurt the baby? That's her trump card. Ge'er has always enjoyed a drink, especially during the times when she's not writing – those periods she refers to as the lacunae of her soul. She can get through a bottle of red wine a day, more if she's out for dinner. She holds her liquor well enough that it's hard to tell when she's drunk, though I've been with her long enough that I know if she's had so much as a glass. Not that I can say exactly what changes, it's more that every individual has their own connection to the world, and hers shifts the instant she starts drinking, like a Bluetooth speaker moving too far from the phone. Be careful of that Huang fella, I say. He's crooked, always ducking and diving. For all we know they're tapping his phone. Make sure you don't get dragged in. It's fine to play ping-pong along the edge of the table, but if you keep using your forehand smash, someone's going to take you out sooner or later. Relax, she says. It's all going to turn out fine. I'll be more or less done with the book by the time the baby arrives, and then I'll be nothing but a mother for a couple of years. If I can even bear to let you do that, I say. Let's have dinner.

Yue Xiaoqi calls again at half past eleven, and this time I answer. Why weren't you at soccer? I ask. We ended up with an odd number of players. Bro, he says, I'm downstairs. Downstairs from my place? I say. Why? I need to talk to you, he says. Can you make some time? He sounds drunk, though still on an even keel, not yet in the trough of despair. Ge'er is in bed. We've been in separate rooms recently because she sleeps so fitfully. Sometimes she'll nap from afternoon to midnight, leap out of bed to grab a pen, look all around her, put the pen back down and fall asleep again. I'm not a particularly light sleeper, but when I get woken up like that it's hard for me to drop off again, and then the next day is a write-off. Now I sleep in the room where the helper used to be. The cot stands ready next to the bed, its bare boards like exposed ribs, still reeking of paint from Shenzhen. I think of the stunt double who died. He was only nineteen, a professional diver. He drowned (to be accurate, he had a heart attack while underwater, and that was it for him). I emerge from my room and gently push Ge'er's door open. Her face is nestled into her shoulder, making her look a little like a gourd. I call her name. Nothing. I shut the door, throw on some clothes and go downstairs.

It's late December and the brisk night air feels

good after the stuffiness of the apartment. The game today has left my body feeling lithe and young. Xiaoqi is smoking by the gate, his back to me, a blue scarf around his neck. He's not bad looking, a typical northern man: tall, square-faced, jowly, long torso, short legs. He's played so much soccer that even just standing there his legs joggle like bedsprings. He used to be an athlete, on the national team for middle- and long-distance running, then somehow he wound up in the arts. He was an actor for five or six years, first as an extra, then a featured extra, eventually graduating to minor TV roles like the female lead's little brother, the sort of character who's always storming out of rooms shouting, Sis, I forbid it! He hasn't been acting much recently. He was the executive director of two low-budget films that neither earned nor lost money but made the rounds of the festivals, not a bad result. Sometimes people say to him, Xiaoqi, weren't you doing well as an actor? You went from playing the female lead's cousin to playing her little brother. Why mess around with movies? They're exhausting and won't make you rich. Hey, there's nothing wrong with movies, he replies. Don't underestimate me. I'll make a real go of this, I'm sure of it. After all, I grew up watching *Landmine Warfare*. Xiaoqi is from the northeast, but after many years in the capital as an actor, he's picked up a strong Beijing accent. Now he calls everyone 'bro' and shakes his head while sighing, What can I do, who asked me to be so fond of you?

He hands me a cigarette. How's Ge'er? he asks. You fighting?

– Not if I do as I'm told. So, what do you want? How do you know where I live anyway?

– It's a long story. Let's find a place to sit down.

– Let's stay here. Ge'er will be frightened if she wakes up and I'm not around.

Xiaoqi looks up and, staring into my eyes, says, It's life and death, bro. This will take two or three hours, but I'll owe you for the rest of my life. He's squinting and his nose is running. His neglected cigarette slowly becomes a column of ash. Looking more closely, I realize he's wearing a coat over pyjamas and no socks: I can see his bare ankles.

– Where should we go?

– Si'de Park. It's quiet there.

– I was just there this afternoon.

– I know. That's why I picked it – it's a place we both know.

Along the way he stops at a supermarket to buy a bottle of blended whiskey and cadges a couple of paper cups from the clerk. I've never been to Si'de Park at night. I'd imagined it would be empty, but a man of indeterminate age wearing a mask and a cap is in the middle of the field doing keep-ups. He's no good – he keeps dropping the ball, but each time he stubbornly hooks it back up with his foot and keeps going. His problem is a lack of coordination. His arms flap by his side and he can't make the ball spin, it just rises and falls like a stone. I watch through the net of the goal and wish I could advise him to stop spending money on soccer shoes, he should just jog around the park instead. I don't actually say anything, of course, even though his arms remind me of a fat duck waddling.

I don't really know Xiaoqi, we've only met a few times at filmmakers' kickabouts. He's quite good at soccer and usually joins the group for beer afterwards, but I've never hung out with him alone. We're both from the northeast, him Changchun and me Shenyang. After a couple of drinks we often end up talking about our hometowns, which I guess brought us a little closer. I heard you were in a gang? he once asked. Only when I was a kid, I said, which doesn't count. I robbed slot machines for them. I've been to Shenyang, he said. It's fine, no major disasters. My grandfather died there during the siege.

53

We sit on a bench. Go ahead, I say. How did you know where I live? The bench we're sitting on is one I've passed by many times, but this is my first time on it. Usually it's occupied by sneaker-wearing old people who bring their own cushions. Si'de Lake ahead of us, grass behind.

– I asked around.

– I see. And how did you know my wife's name?

– I asked about that too while I was at it. Also, you posted about her. You treat her really well, you're spoiling her.

– I think we're straying from the point.

– I have a question.

– Ask away.

– I know we're not close, and it's a bit cheeky of me to ask, but why did you come with me?

– You said it was life and death.

– My life and my death. That's still my business, not yours. The streets are full of people with life-and-death problems. Look at the beggars with small children singing on the subway. Real or not, that's still a matter of life and death.

– I may not know you well, but we respect each other and I've always had a good impression of you. Besides, we're from the same region. That's why I came downstairs. If you're just drunk and bored, go find a police officer to amuse yourself with, and I'll go back to Ge'er.

He hands me the paper cup.

– I thought of going to the police too, but I wanted to ask your opinion first. Drink?

– Just a drop.

– All right. Warm yourself up. Not too sweet, is it?

– What is it you want to tell me.

– Let me pour you some more. Don't drink if you don't want to, I just hate seeing someone with an empty cup. It's like this, I was a bit of a jock when I was young, didn't do much book-learning, but I did have one skill: ever since I was little, I could tell with one look whether someone was reliable or not. And bro, I feel like I can count on you. That's why you were the first person who came to mind. I've been in Beijing over ten years, but tonight I couldn't think of a single person other than you. You remind me of a guy from my track team: a little shorter than me, stuttered, but could run really fast and always had my back in a fight. The coach made him lift weights and he snapped a tendon. Never saw him again. The first time I saw you I thought you sounded a bit like him. But you couldn't possibly be him, I guess.

– Right. I couldn't be, I'm in the arts.

–You're not him. You make the same facial expressions when you talk but the words are different. You're better than him at faking it. Bro, listen, I got into a fight with my wife just now and accidentally beat her to death.

I jump to my feet and yelp, Don't joke like that!

I have two kids, he continues, a boy and a girl. She's six and he's four. They're sound asleep in their bunk beds right now. The girl has the top bunk. He reaches into his jacket pocket and brings out an ancient-looking bronze dagger, two-inch handle and foot-long blade, no trace of blood. I got this while I was filming in Xi'an, he says. Gift from a friend, it's the real thing. Don't worry, I didn't stab her or anything, I hit her with the handle. He raps the knife against his palm. Just like that, whap, ten times.

I look around. It's not totally dark, here and there bushes are visible in the gloom, and I can see a building in the distance, a huge sign on top. I place a hand on his shoulder and say, Xiaoqi. He sighs. Thank you for trusting me, I say. Please put that thing away. I'll go to the police station with you. A domestic squabble got out of hand, that's all. I'll find someone to get you out of this, it's really no big deal. He looks up at me, gets to his feet, and with a flick of his hand sends the dagger into the long grass.

No way, he says. If I wanted to go to the police I would have driven there myself. It's not that I don't want to pay for what I did, but I have a bellyful of words I can't say to the cops.

My phone pings with a message from Ge'er: *Where are you?*

Xiaoqi pours himself another half cup and says, Go ahead and answer, I'm in no rush.

I reply: *Nearby, with a friend.* Then unsend it and instead type: *Nearby. An old classmate had something urgent come up. Go back to sleep babe.*

Her: *An old classmate from when?*

Me: *Junior high. Haven't seen him in a while. He insisted on meeting.*

Her: *Okay, have a nice chat. I'm not tired, I'll write a bit more. Where's the Murakami mixtape?*

(I'd made her a CD of every piece of music mentioned in Murakami's books.)

Me: *Drawer of the right-hand bedside table in the spare room. The CD tray gets stuck sometimes, pull it out with your fingers if you need to.*

Her: *Our little one is being quiet, don't worry. If you're drinking make sure you pick up the tab, don't let your friend spend his money.*

Me: *Let's see how much we get through. Happy writing.*

There's a haze in the night air that I feel rather than see. It gets into my lungs, chills me from the inside, it's in my eyes like dandruff. I recall walking down the stairs, watching Xiaoqi buy the booze, sitting here, drinking – why did I do all that? Who is this guy anyway? Not family, not a close friend, just someone who passed me the ball a few times with reasonable skill. I only converted a couple of those passes into goals, but I always gave him a thumbs up after. A perpetually smiling midfielder, a left wing with a good eye.

I turn to him: Where's the body?

– Your wife worried?

– Never mind about her. Where's the body?

– In my trunk. My car's by the park entrance, we passed it earlier.

– So, was it an accident?

– Hitting her was on purpose, killing her was an accident.

– Have you thought of killing her before?

– It's crossed my mind.

I stare at him in silence.

– I wasn't planning to kill her *this* time.

– Were you cheating on her?

– No. We've been married seven years and I've never cheated, not once.

– You can't get it up?

– Not to brag, but I'm definitely better in that department than most people.

– How much money did she leave you?

– Nothing. I earned all our money. Her parents got laid off.

– Then why did you want to kill her?

– It was an accident.

– I know, but you said you wanted to kill her before. Why?

– We grew up on Guilin Road in Changchun. Do you know it?

– No.

– It's a chaotic place. We've known each other twenty-five years. Just imagine. Back in the day, everyone went skating at the northside rink. That's where I met her. She was really good, led every conga line. I always pushed to the front so I could hold her waist. Finally she swung around and said, You again? I'm Yue Xiaoqi, I said. I'm at Eleventh High, and I do track and field. They gave us some canned beef Monday, you want some? I don't know you, she said. Why would I want your canned beef? You know me now, don't you? I said. What's your name? Yang Buhui, she said. Yang Buhui? I repeated. You don't know who Yang Buhui is? she asked. Isn't that you? I said. That amused her. That's a character from *The Heaven Sword and Dragon Saber*. Don't you have a TV? Yes, I said, but it's not hooked up. It was a novel before it was a TV show, she said. Don't you read? I want to, I said, but it makes me sleepy. I enjoy it, though. Yang as in the surname, Buhui as in no regrets, she said. Hold on tight, let's shake off our tail. She pivoted sharply and the less experienced skaters behind us went flying into the side of the rink, as if we were a whip lashing the wall.

As Xiaoqi tells the story, he mimes skating. Through the gloom I see his hands on Yang Buhui's waist, head bent so he can talk to her. He stumbles at the curve, but manages not to let go. Past the turn he can relax.

Xiaoqi returns from the ice rink to the bench.

– I killed her because she's sick.

– Sick with what?

– She's always up at night.

– What do you mean?

– When it started, she'd get out of bed and spend a long time in the bathroom. In the morning I'd find her asleep on the toilet, lipstick in her hand. Then it was sticking photos on the wall, pictures of us from when we first met up to now. I'd find her asleep on the floor. When I asked her about it the next day, she wouldn't remember a thing. Really? I'd say, and she'd say yes, not a thing. I know her, she wouldn't lie. After that she started showing up at the train station, no idea where she wanted to go, just walking around the station. Whenever she saw someone, she'd say, Have you seen the Bright Left Messenger?

– What, as in Yang Buhui's father?

– Yes, him.

– Sorry if this is a rude question, but when she went out like this, was she dressed?

– Fully dressed. Sometimes she got mixed up, like one time she wore our daughter's scarf, then walked the five kilometres there and insisted on crawling into the luggage-screening machine. Drink that. Look, it's starting to soak into the cup.

My phone pings again. I step aside to check it. It's Ge'er: *Detective Huang faxed to say he's found sixteen victims in Xinjiang, Shandong, Xi'an and Sichuan. He has statements. People he met online, prostitutes, old classmates. Five of them will never be able to have children. One of them got a high fever and lost all hearing in her left ear. The perp finally talked tonight. Detective Huang's mole will get me a transcript. This is going to be the core of my novel. I need a drink.*

I glance at the time on my phone: 1.10. I text: *Have a glass of red wine.*

Her: *Deal. Where are you?*

Me: *A bar. Not much going on. They're closing soon.*

Her: *What are you talking about?*

Me: *Just the past. We don't have much else in common. The time he scored an own goal at a school match and cried all afternoon. That sort of thing.*

She sends me a hug emoji, a tiny monk-like man with green arms that look like balls.

Xiaoqi pisses into the grass. I pour myself some whiskey, down it and pour myself some more. I try to work out where we can go for more booze once we finish.

He shakes himself off and comes back to me. There's someone playing ball over there, he says, pointing.

– Yes, the guy's half-crippled.

– Maybe playing keep-up will fix him. Now I think about it, maybe I'm the one responsible for my wife's sickness.

– How so?

– She caught me jerking off while she was asleep once.

– I don't know about that.

– I didn't do it on purpose or anything, I was just bored. Sometimes I jerk off three times a night. Rely on no one but yourself, I say. Just like those people who said they'd starve to death before they touched American rations.

    – Was it really like that?

    – Bro, I wrapped my wife in plastic.

    – Why?

    – She loves things to be clean. Everything in the fridge is covered in cling film. I took her to see the doctor but he said there's nothing wrong with her, she's even healthier than me. She's tried not falling asleep, but that's impossible. I need sleep too, I need to work during the day to raise our two kids.

    – Did you ever think about locking her up? I mean at night.

He nods: Of course, but then she blinded herself in one eye. I found her before she could do the other one. After that I stopped working and just followed her around at night. I thought maybe one day she'd grow tired and stop; we just hadn't gone round the curve yet. But then she lost an eye.

A stray cat sashays elegantly past us. She's on the prowl for a mate, says Xiaoqi. He flicks his cigarette butt, sending a shower of sparks through the air. The cat nimbly dodges it and minces away along the lakeshore. The soccer player is taking a water break, arms resting on one outstretched leg.

The furthest she's ever been is Longguan, says

Xiaoqi. When she's out roaming at night, she doesn't recognize anyone, not even me. She skips along, humming tunes.

– Which tunes?

– Children's songs. I thought she might be homesick, so we made a trip to Changchun. Her ma's dead, and her ba shacked up with another woman. He was shocked to see her missing an eye. They didn't talk much. She was kind of numb – no childhood nostalgia there – but she kept slipping her ba spending money. I pretended not to notice. I asked her ba to sing her a nursery rhyme. He thought I was insane, so I beat him up and we came back home.

Xiaoqi tips some of the booze from my cup into his.

– She looks younger at night. She's always smiling. She hasn't worked for a few years now, since she was raising the kids. She's done a good job with them. Do you know my son can recite over a hundred Tang poems?

I grunt noncommittally.

– She's gained thirty jin in the time I've known her. Her ass is huge. Sometimes, coming out of the shower, when she puts on her knickers it looks like she's stepping into a cooking pot. One night I got drunk and didn't notice her leaving the house. She had our daughter on her back. When I caught up with them they were playing hide-and-seek in the middle of the road. I called my daughter over and hugged her. Is she yours? my wife asked. Can I play with her a little longer? I promise not to hide under any other cars. That's when I decided that she couldn't go on living.

– You could have had her committed. You could have gotten her help. I guess it's no use saying this now.

– And let her gouge out her other eye? Or bite off her own tongue? Or be raped by psychos? What if she started losing her mind in the daytime, when she was lucid, because she missed the kids so badly? Bro, there's not much I could do. Maybe my uselessness put her in this state, and now I've taken her out of it.

He stands, tosses his cup in the air and kicks it into the fence. He does some leg-raises.

– My daughter wanted to have a serious talk about all this with me. Her ma fell ill when she was five and a half, and she's seven now. She told me she wished her ma would vanish.

– Your daughter?

– Yes. She was sure her ma had become a different

65

person, so why not let her disappear and get a new ma? Strange mothers are all the same anyway.

– And what does your son think?

– He wanted to keep taking care of her. He'd give her his newest toys, he'd put Band-Aids on her feet when they're cut up from nightwalking. But it was two to one. He was outvoted.

I glance at my phone. Ge'er texted twenty minutes ago: *Okay, here's my hypothesis. One possibility is this guy has a terminal disease, and his wife left him, or maybe she slept with a co-worker of his, so now he believes all women are whores. A bit Hollywood, but sometimes life imitates art. Or else he adores his wife but she's dead, and they never had any kids, so now he thinks no other women deserve children, since a woman as good as his wife couldn't have them. What do you think?*

She's definitely had more than one glass of wine, is what I think. When Ge'er is drunk, her face blooms red like the scarlet-veiled rabbit demon in *Journey to the West*. She also gets very formal and earnest, as if nothing matters in the world except her opinion on this particular issue.

A second message arrives five minutes later: *Detective Huang sent over the perp's first statement. He's been married for decades, two kids (one in the US, one in Shanghai), wife is a radiologist, still alive. No problems with the marriage. They go for evening strolls and weekend bike rides through the countryside. He likes to cook and he's good at it, mostly Hangzhou cuisine. When they started questioning him he gave detailed recipes for some of his favourite dishes, then went quiet. That's going to be the opening of my novel. I feel like he's balding, though I need to confirm with Detective Huang. I'm thinking multiple storylines, omniscient perspective, the intertwining narratives of victims and perpetrator that intersect halfway through, then the second part is the investigation and trial. If you have any suggestions, make them quickly. Once I start writing, I'll be set on that path. And if you have a drink in front of you right now, I recommend leaving it. You always have exactly one glass too many. Restraint is a virtue, whether in art or in life.*

There isn't a drop of whiskey left, but it feels inappropriate to suggest finding another place to drink. The alcohol is slowly taking effect. I feel comforted, weary. Everything seems ridiculous, but also understandable. Xiaoqi is less affected, still tipsily good-natured and full of energy.

– What now, bro? Why did you come to me?

– I needed someone I could trust. Help me bury her. Then if I die, at least someone else will know where she is.

– Where do we do it?

– I wanted to ask your opinion. Do you think this park would work? Maybe by the lake?

– Not here. I play ball here all the time.

– Further away then. Shunyi maybe, or Tongzhou. I'm just worried that one day there'll be construction and they'll dig her up.

– I have a question. Isn't someone going to notice she's missing? She has friends and family, doesn't she?

– The police know about her illness. I'll report her missing. The owner of my building is in a fight with the management company, so all the security cameras have been turned off.

– That's why you chose this moment.

– I thought I'd give it a try. I didn't expect it to work the first time. This is just like when we decided to have a child.

– What kind of car do you have?

– A Subaru.

– Fine. I'm going to have a piss, then we can find a place. You came to the right person, by the way. I'm from the northeast, so we're brothers. 'For ten years now the living and dead have been parted' – you get me?

– Slow down, bro, he says.

– Don't touch anything. You don't want to leave any fingerprints. Let me handle everything. No one will suspect me. You're clever to have picked me. To be honest, I've been drifting away from my friends all these years. I've been waiting for a chance to help someone out like this. You get me. You see me. Hang on while I pee.

I walk into the long grass and let rip. It's as cold as it's going to get and my piss melts the frost as it spatters the undergrowth. Twenty years ago, I'd often be out with my crew at this time of night. If a woman walked by we'd escort her home, bantering all the way to her corner, then we'd sit back down on the sidewalk and shoot the breeze. I didn't like going home. My parents were always fighting, and my ba used to put my ma in hospital. She was at fault too, but so what? I tried to step in but I could never beat him, couldn't reach far enough to land a punch on his head. By the time I was old enough to match him, he'd gotten ill and died. That old saying about revenge being best served cold? Bullcrap. After peeing, I crouch down and hunt around until I find the dagger behind a bush. I wrap the blade in my scarf, take off my shoes and hold them in my other hand, then sneak around in a big arc until I'm behind Xiaoqi. He's sitting with his hands on his knees, as if he's thinking over what I just said. I aim for his head, and try to recall the proper stance, which reminds me of chopping garlic for my ma as a kid. I touch the back of my own head and have a sudden flashback to my wedding vows, not the actual words but this moment when we were both sobbing like we might never stop. That threw the officiant off, and the rest of the ceremony was a mess. I bring the handle of the dagger down hard, then Xiaoqi is on the ground. I roll him over. He's still breathing, probably won't be out long. I feel the back of his head. His skull is still intact. I lift him back up onto the bench, cover him with my jacket and get his car keys from his pocket. After a moment's thought I place the empty whiskey bottle in his hand.

The soccer player has started up again, left leg right leg left leg. The ball refuses to cooperate, keeps slipping off his foot as if it's been greased. I put my shoes back on, open the gate and walk out onto the pitch. He turns to look at me, and for the first time I see him clearly. Fifteen or sixteen, red headphones, pasty white face, eyebrows that look trimmed. The ball rolls past me. I pick it up and knee it a couple of times. Even though I've been drinking, I've still got my balance. I manage over twenty keep-ups before letting it fall beneath my foot, where I puncture it with the dagger. I toss the deflated ball to the teen-ager and walk back out the gate.

It takes some time to find the car – Xiaoqi parked further away than I expected, down an alleyway. I hesitate, then get in without looking in the trunk. A ping. Ge'er has texted: *Detective Huang says the perp killed himself. He had a poison capsule hidden in a false tooth. No one knows why he did it or how many victims there actually were. How many women are out there not even knowing they can no longer have kids? Did he hate all women? How did he choose his victims? Did these women do something wrong? Was he working to some kind of debt sheet given to him by god? My novel is ruined, and I've started bleeding. That's not a meta-phor, it's actually happening. I'm not in any pain, don't worry, it's just a little blood. I can feel a part of me, like a rib, tumbling out into the filthy flood of life. He doesn't know what's happening, he doesn't feel any fear. Raise a glass to him. I'm waiting for you.*

I start the car and drive home. The tank is full. There's a red booster seat next to me. The Subaru's pedal is loose, and I have to step down hard on it. It takes about three minutes to get to our building. I get out, walk around the car, and summon the courage I'll need to open the trunk. If it's empty, I'll drive Ge'er to hospital, then go back to the park for Xiaoqi. Inside the trunk is a woman in a pink nightie, wrapped in clear plastic with only her head poking out. Her hands are clasped before her chest and her hair is loose. No make-up. Her face is as placid as a pasture in winter. White eye patch over one eye. I take a deep breath, then like a midwife I lift her from the trunk. She's on the plump side, but lighter than I expected. Where am I taking her? I have no idea now why I picked her up. Her body is still warm. Her arms dangle loosely. Where do you want to go? I mumble. Out of nowhere she gasps for air. Gunk spews from her mouth and her nose starts bleeding. Her good eye blinks open and she looks at me. Great, she says. What? I say. It's great, this winter. And you – She reaches out and gently strokes my nose. You'll never know how long it took me to walk here, but I have no regrets. And then, with all the strength in her body, she lets out a sob like a thunderclap.

Theatre

AFTER GRADUATING FROM COLLEGE I CAME
back to S——— and got a job at our local TV
station, which has five channels – News, Drama,
Sports, Entertainment and Education – serving the
city's two million people and another three hundred
thousand in satellite towns. People further afield
can't watch our programmes no matter how much
they might enjoy them. I worked in News with seven
or eight others, half men and half women. I regarded
them all as nonentities and I'm sure they saw me
the same way, which helped us get along. They did
their thing, I did mine, and we left each other alone.
After work, they stayed late in the office and played
Murder with an old pack of cards. Apparently this
helped them bond. Sometimes I looked back from
the gate and saw the lights still on in the office, all
of them sitting around the long white table bluffing
and accusing each other. I'd pick up my pace and

turn down the next alleyway, trying to get to a place where I could no longer see the lights.

I often wonder where my solitary nature comes from. My parents were introverted too; we never had visitors as far back as I can remember. On the rare occasions when the electricity-bill collector came knocking at our door, we'd tense up as if someone had lifted our bedclothes to look at the soles of our feet. My parents enforced a clear separation between their jobs, which were merely means of earning money, and our home, which they ran like a top-secret organization. Our apartment only gave the appearance of taking up space in the building; it was really an invisible nothingness, the three of us hidden among the treetops. What secrets did we actually have? My parents were ordinary workers, and they only ever talked about their colleagues, miscellany from the factory and the accumulated grievances of our clan. They cooked ordinary meals: long beans with noodles, greens and meatball soup, steamed egg for breakfast. No secret recipes. Their savings account held so little money it wasn't worth mentioning, and they didn't own much jewellery. Their most valuable possession was probably a gold ring my grandma left my ma, which had a coppery gleam and bore visible toothmarks. It was hard to understand why they were so reclusive. It wasn't poverty – everyone in our tenement was as poor as we were. I promise you there weren't any secret millionaires living there under assumed names. Our neighbours were always in and out of each other's pockets. They were always asking one another for help, or getting into arguments and ambushing each other. My parents were the only ones who kept their front door shut and lived their own lives, even though they didn't have agoraphobia or any kidnapped children they needed to keep hidden away. I could never understand it.

I didn't move back in with them after returning to S———; instead, I rented a small flat near the TV station. Habit is a fearsome thing, and though I've believed in my own wisdom since I was a child, understanding from the age of ten or so that the way my parents lived was unacceptable and a little laughable, when I started living on my own I realized I'd absorbed some of their faults. The first thing I did after moving in was change the locks. My rental was a fifty-six-square-metre one-bedroom belonging to a civil servant who owned seven or eight similar properties in S———. He did them all up the same way, like a hotel that had accidentally scattered its rooms across the city. I was on the seventh floor, and my window looked out onto the rear of a nearby building that resembled a backbone, one vertebra stacked atop another – the TV station's new office block. Because of the obstructed view, my rent was two-thirds that of similar flats in the neighbour-hood. After moving in I realized that although I got no light at dawn and needed to set my alarm clock, the setting sun filtered through the building's spine, bursting straight through my window and venturing into my flat. No one assessing my place from a conventional point of view would recognize this as an asset, but as the saying goes: one's true nature always shows itself in time. I bought a pot of daffo-dils and placed them right where the sunlight fell, and needless to say they thrived. In fact, they did so well I soon got bored with them and bought some roses too.

About a month after starting work at the station, I celebrated my twenty-fourth birthday (it was September, I'm a Virgo). The evening before, I was handed an assignment to take pictures of old people exercising in Laodong Park. Well, more of a prac-tice task than an assignment. The footage would be turned into a five-minute film. I got up very early and arrived at the park before dawn. Already there was someone stretching, though he wasn't particularly old, maybe in his forties. With a kick, he swung his leg up to rest on a tree branch. Nearby, a woman in her fifties was futzing around with an accordion, like she was trying to harness it to her head. I set up my tripod, aimed the camera at them, and stood to one side smoking. The man kept staring at me. When he was done stretching he said, Hey, what are you up to?

I'm from the TV station, I said, sucking deeply on my cigarette out of nervousness, almost swallowing the damn thing.

– Oh, I see. So I'm on your radar?

– Yes. Can we begin?

– Sure. I'll start with a Six Harmonies sequence.

– Great, we can go from there.

The man went through his boxing practice then turned to swordplay, his movements clean and precise, eyes blazing, sword tassels grazing his face every now and then. When he stopped for a drink of water the woman started playing her accordion. I'm not done, the man said, but she ignored him.

Why had I come back to work in S——? Two reasons: first, after getting a literature degree in Beijing, I realized there was nowhere to go from there. Anything I did would involve living like an ant, forced to carry loads several times my body weight.

I'd actually wanted to study law, but I was placed in the literature department instead because my grades weren't good enough. It didn't seem worth the effort either to continue on this path or to start over from scratch. I still had more than thirty yuan on my travel card, so I roamed around on the subway till the card was empty, then I dropped it in a trash can. Second, I had a friend in S—— called Cao Xixue. We grew up in the same tenement block and she was the only person I got on with. From when I was five or six, we'd talk about all kinds of things whenever we got together. She's three years older than me and studied at a local college, then got a job at a bank in S——. Shortly before I graduated she sent me a letter to say she'd been doing well for the last few years. She got married along the way and divorced a few months later. Her life was very full. If I was having fun in Beijing she'd come visit, but just to be sure, maybe I should come back to S—— to have a look – there'd been a lot of construction in recent years and the place looked completely different. There was no romantic spark between us, so I tended to trust what she said.

The woman's accordion-playing was very resonant. Behind her, another woman started singing into a mic attached to a black speaker; it went staticky and quivered whenever she hit a high note. Leaving aside the equipment malfunction, her voice was pretty good. I smoked as I watch her. She was maybe fifty-seven or so, fairly slim, white hair under a hairnet, tallish – I would guess 170 centimetres – dressed in a reasonably clean cream dress, brown shoes and cream ankle socks. I listened to three songs, realized the next ten songs would be exactly the same, turned off the camera and got a taxi home. I was still on probation, so my boss wasn't too strict with me. I could say I was filming all day, and that would be okay as long as I had some footage to show for it.

When I was at college – in my third year, to be precise – the tenement block I grew up in caught fire because a perpetually unemployed guy who was trying to become an inventor created a substance that made petrol even more flammable. One night, his invention set his bedding alight, followed by the thin partition separating his flat from the next. The flames swiftly spread across the building's frame. A survivor said it burned like a rolled-up newspaper. In an hour there was nothing left. The would-be inventor died from smoke inhalation – he was found by his window, which he hadn't managed to get open. Twelve other people were killed, and nine were badly injured. It was deep winter and everyone was wearing woollen clothing, the sort that bursts into flames at the slightest spark, turning its wearers into giant fireballs and melting into their skin. Some families had been using 'little suns' – cheap space heaters – that exploded in the chaos, sending their metal frames crashing through the windows onto the street below. I can imagine our apartment catching fire, the flames unwanted guests in a place that had never seen visitors. My parents' immediate reaction was probably to try to save their few possessions, not that it mattered because the inventor lived next door to them, so they were at the heart of the conflagration. Even the firemen didn't think they could survive. Strangely, they didn't end up trapped, but were flung from the fourth floor by the explosion. At the crucial moment they abandoned their home and went flying through the air, my father still clutching my mother's reading glasses. They suffered broken bones and concussions, and my father was left with a permanent limp, but they survived and returned to their previous lifestyle, becoming shut-ins at a different location. They almost never mentioned the fire, and when relatives asked, they replied, It was just like they said on the news. I felt extremely guilty about not being there, though I knew my presence wouldn't necessarily have led to a better outcome.

Back home, I lay in bed flipping through a book before dozing off. As the glow of the setting sun seeped through the window, I watered the daffodils and repositioned them so the light hit their long, slender leaves. Just before dusk Xixue phoned and asked if I'd like to come out. I still hadn't seen her since I'd returned – she'd been busy. I got dressed and headed to the place she named, which was quite remote. It took forty minutes to get there, and by the end the driver and I were the only people left on the bus. Xixue was waiting for me at the Sitaizi stop. It had somehow been years since we'd seen each other, though we'd spoken on the phone and exchanged letters. She was older, of course, and her eyes were more deep-set than before. Like her ba's. I took in her oddly proportioned body (long neck, wide hips, short legs, making her look like a pear) and attractive features (aquiline nose, small mouth, melon-seed face). If not for her dark, blemished skin, she could have passed for a white Russian émigrée. For as long as I'd known her, she'd been great at expressing herself, and frequently left me at a loss for words. Her marvellous mouth almost seemed to control her brain rather than vice versa. Even when she didn't know what to say, she only had to open her mouth and the words came flying out. This caused its own problems, of course. She was incapable of keeping secrets, because she'd say anything to anyone. Out of all the people I'd ever met, she was the only one who did this. I found it a good habit, because it was something I lacked myself. There were so many things I didn't wish to talk about that I often ended up lying to her, but she never minded. Even when I contradicted myself, she wouldn't poke holes in my story. I came across as slow-witted and honest, but actually I told more lies than anyone I knew. As for Xixue, she talked a lot but every word was true. An extraordinary person.

She had her hair in a bun. I'd never seen her wear it like this before. It made her neck look longer, a handle you could pick her up by. What took you so long? she asked.

– I had to wait fifteen minutes for the bus. Then we clipped a van and I had to wait for another bus.

– We've got a metro now. Why didn't you just take that? Subway trains don't get into accidents. You've lost a ton of weight. What are you even eating? And when did you get an ear stud? It's hideous, you look like a gangster. Not a motorbike gangster, more electric scooter. I've been so busy I didn't have time to get you a birthday present, you don't mind, do you? Better if your birthday were next month.

– No worries. Why are we meeting in the middle of nowhere?

– Come with me. It's a bit deserted here, but it's livelier up ahead.

I followed her along the side of the road, past a slim railway track, but it remained just as deserted as before.

After twenty minutes we arrived at a two-storey building: a door below, two windows above, nothing else around. Or not quite nothing – I could make out the traces of demolished houses, like the dusty squares left behind after moving furniture. The outer walls of the building were greyish white, fanning outwards as they extended to the rear. It wasn't just the neighbouring houses that had been torn down, I realized, but every structure within a square kilometre or so, leaving just this trapezoid. This is my friend's place, said Xixue. She's out of the country so I'm taking care of it for her. On vacation? I asked. No, permanently, she's given up. Look at this door – it's from the thirties. How long are you going to do this? I asked. It depends, she said. I don't know her very well.

Xixue opened the door with a long black key. It was pitch dark inside until she turned on the light, revealing a theatre. There was a wooden stage up front, about thirty metres by ten, framed by curtains. The audience seating had gone yellowish, the same shade as the gunk on my tongue first thing in the morning. I live upstairs, she said, though the ceiling's so low it's hard to stand upright.

– What are you doing here? Do you work nearby?

– My office is fifteen kilometres away. I have to ride my bike to the metro station every morning. Look at this wall, touch it, feel the bullet holes – a warlord once fired on this place because of a play.

– You haven't answered me. What are you doing here?

– Isn't it obvious? I rehearse every day. This is private property, and it's old enough that the government isn't allowed to tear it down. They didn't realize that before clearing the rest of the district, but now they've had to halt the demolition. Who knows what's going to happen next, but I can use it for now.

– When did you start acting? You've never mentioned it before. And who are you acting for?

– It's my new hobby. I started when I got the place. Give me any size of shoe and I'll make sure my feet fit, understand? There's no audience. I'm just acting for myself. Why leave such a magnificent stage empty? Don't you ever feel like that? It's like seeing the ocean and knowing you have to get in, whether or not you know how to swim. That kind of feeling.

I stared at Xixue. She hadn't changed one bit. I understood why she'd avoided me for so many years. Her father, the inventor, burned all those people to death and left my father lame. Of course she didn't want to see me, but at least she kept writing letters. She always had so much to say, but she hadn't mentioned her father, and she hadn't apologized, but then why should she? She was her father's child, not the other way round. Looking closely at her mouth, I realized she'd changed – she was more stubborn, fiercer in her self-belief. She used to pause for breath amid her torrents of speech, but now everything blurted out in one go, her lips moving at the speed of light until her lungs were completely empty. She wrote in one of her letters that for a couple of years she swam a few thousand metres a day. Sure enough, her shoulders were broad as a man's, and her neck was much thicker. Water beats fire, I guess. She also mentioned she'd spent more than a year volunteering at her local library, which left her with quite a few calluses. Then the building was demolished and the books were absorbed by the municipal library. They cut down her volunteer hours, so she quit and got a job at Shashan Church. She lasted less than a year there because she wasn't religious and hated organized rituals.

– My bed isn't made so I won't invite you upstairs.

– That's fine. Can you cook here?

– No, there's no water or electricity. I've set up a generator, though, because lighting is the guts of theatre.

– You're unbelievable.

– It may sound like a lot of effort, but actually it wasn't difficult at all. Are you hungry? We can go get some food nearby, though I don't usually eat dinner.

I lied: Me neither, I gained six or seven jin after graduating and none of my trousers fit any more. What play are you putting on?

– Good question. I've done a lot of Shakespeare and Chekhov, obviously not on my own – I have quite a few actors at my disposal. I want to do some new writing next.

– Wait, there are other actors?

– Obviously. I'd lose my mind if I was acting all on my own. I invited you here because I want you to write us a script.

– That's not in my stars. Since when am I a playwright? I haven't even read Shakespeare or Chekhov.

– Didn't you study literature? I don't know fancy sayings like the one you just used. You can write.

– Studying is different to writing. I'm not interested in that stuff anyway. You know how many people study politics every year? And how many of them get to be president?

– You can write. I'm never wrong about people. You've told lies ever since you were a kid, so coming up with a script should be no problem. Just put your effort into that instead of playing dumb. I've studied you for a long time. You can't do anything, but you do have a talent for playwriting. Just sit there, smack your head and let the words flow out. The other actors will be here soon – you can watch us rehearse for inspiration.

– But I'm – how can I put this? My head is spinning.

– You're dizzy?

– Yes, I can't catch my breath. All the strength has gone out of my body. Could you stop moving? I'm seeing double, I feel like vomiting every time you move. I need to go home.

– Don't you like it here?

– It's not that, I really am feeling ill. I haven't eaten all day and the bus was stuffy as hell. Let's talk another day. I can't stand the bus, I'll get a taxi home.

Xixue tilted her head to one side and stared at me as if she'd just found a cave and was trying to figure out if there were wolves inside. After a few seconds she said, Okay, I can see you're not well, go on home. We rehearse at seven every Tuesday and Wednesday, come along if you're free. I patted her on the arm and staggered out through the thick wooden doors.

It was dark outside. I got a taxi home, my head spinning. That place was shut up tight, the large windows locked, the floor all dusty, and the screws on the chairs gave off a weird smell. Back home, I found some fried steamed buns in the kitchen and headed to bed after I'd eaten, even though it wasn't yet nine.

I slept a very long time and felt amazing when I woke up, as if I'd grown during the night. The spine outside blocked all the harassing light, and I stayed in bed until I felt completely lucid. I arrived at the station after ten and handed the tape to my boss, who'd already watched six or seven of these practice reels. The atmosphere in the screening room was solemn, and my comrades were standing around like traitors waiting to be expelled. Not only was I late, I realized, but I'd failed to edit my footage at all. Every other reel featured close-ups, music, voice-overs in pleasingly low tones. Were you on assignment last night? asked my boss. No, I said. Then why are you only arriving now? he said. A childhood friend fell down a well, I said. I went to make sure she was all right. He glared at me. What well? The one across from the toyshop on Xinhua Street, I said. She was walking along, talking to me on the phone, then all of a sudden she fell down the well. She knocked out four teeth. I was partly responsible, so I had to go see her. Did you film it? he said. What? I said. Did you film the incident? he said. No, I said. I still don't have a reporter's instinct. I'll reflect on that. Give me your tape, he said. This was also my first time watching it: a man stretching, me asking a few questions, some boxing, a woman playing the accordion while another woman sang three songs. The film ended when the music did. She sang well, which I hadn't realized at the time. I also hadn't noticed she was staring directly at the camera. What was that? said my boss. I wanted to capture the condition of these people, I said. And what condition might that be? he said. Early morning, I said. Is that woman a professional singer? he said. No, I said, but she moved me. Rewind a bit, listen to when she sings *I wait for him like a flower, touch my shoulder and I'll do as you say*. Her voice was unsteady before, but that line came out really well. Okay, he said. I'll have to deal with you, just like the people upstairs have to deal with me. Understand? Take two days off. Leave your camera on the table. I need to think about this.

That night, I went to my parents' place for dinner. Afterwards they played a card game they invented, though I suspect it's based on an existing game. You shuffle two decks and draw cards to see who goes first. The second person has to put down a card that matches the number or suit of the card put down by the first player, or draw a card if they don't have a match. The person with the most cards at the end loses. I watched them play for half an hour before saying goodbye. Outside, I called Xixue but she didn't answer, so I got the metro to Sitaizi and walked twenty minutes to the house, where I spotted two men standing across the road. Both were in long-sleeved shirts, one white and one yellow, and both were wearing belted black trousers. One had a document bag under one arm. They were standing very close together, balding at the temples, watching the house in silence like two strangers at an art gallery viewing the same painting. I watched them for a while, and they stared back at me. After a few minutes I knocked on the door, but there was no answer. I called Xixue again, and this time she answered. I'm at your door, I said. Okay, she said, did you get the metro here? Yes, I said. Are you feeling better? she said. Yes, I said. I wondered if you had low blood sugar, she said. That can be dangerous. Are you alone? Yes, I said, can I come in? All right, I'm coming, she said. Four or five minutes passed before she opened the door. Inside, the stage was lit as brilliantly as a forest fire, and six women were sitting on it. As I came closer, I saw that two of them were roughly Xixue's age and the others were older, though no more than forty. Most of them had their eyes shut, and I realized all of them were blind.

I know them from Shashan Church, said Xixue, coming up next to me. And their families too. Every Tuesday and Wednesday I give them a lift here and get them home before ten. On Sundays they attend the service. We're rehearsing *The Tempest*, you can watch.

I stayed where I was: No thanks.

– Why not? Watching a play doesn't take much energy.

– I don't want to. To be honest, I don't like what you're doing.

– What do you mean?

– This building is too stuffy, and I don't understand *The Tempest*. Who's playing the titular role?

– No one.

– Right, I don't understand that. My father needs a new crutch, I'd better go buy him one.

She turned to look at me: You fucker.

– I've lost my job. I have a lot of time on my hands, maybe I can write you a script. There's seven of you, eight including me. Do you still need one?

– Go home. I see what you're trying to do. We each have a destiny of our own. I'm very tired. Let's not talk about this any more.

– Is this how you're rescuing yourself?

She looked up and smiled. I wish you'd burned to death, she said.

When I walked out, the two men were gone. I noticed a van behind the house – that must be how Xixue transported the actors there and back. Maybe I'd gone too far, but I didn't want to spend a second longer looking at this trapezoidal building. I hurried away.

ACT ONE

An old study. A tall man in his sixties is reading on a chaise longue, dressed in a black robe. A lone flickering candle illuminates his face. His feet rest on a stool and twitch every now and then. There is a knock at the door.

MAN.   Enter.

SERVANT.   Master.

MAN.   How long till we dock? Why are you looking so haggard?

SERVANT.   About seven days. The cities are emptying out. People are fleeing.

MAN.   How many followers are left? I like how quiet the boat is now.

SERVANT.   I'm the only one left. Everyone's scared of the plague, and no one has faith in your divinity like I do.

MAN.   How many times must I tell you? I have no divinity. I'm just visiting my hometown, and if anyone is still alive there I want to speak to them. That's my whole plan. It's getting late, you should sleep. Conserve your energy. Early to bed and early to rise – that's how to avoid the plague.

The servant bows and exits. The man paces. Suddenly the room sways and he almost falls. Sitting back down, he begins reading again with a smile, completely absorbed. The night is deep as an ocean, but he's not drowsy at all. A knock at the door.

MAN.   Enter.

SERVANT.   Master.

MAN.   Why are you still awake? Are you thinking of leaving too?

SERVANT.   If I may be frank, it's too late now to leave even if I wanted to. There's only the vast sea or the plague-ridden docks. I will accompany you to the end.

MAN.   Eat the medicinal herbs we prepared. If we survive, you'll have no end of respect. I'll build a statue of you in your current tormented state.

SERVANT.   A boat is rowing towards us pleading for rescue. Should we allow them to board?

MAN.   Why not? Don't delay, go rescue them.

SERVANT.   If we let them board, they may never leave. What if they have the dreaded plague?

MAN.   What language are they calling for help in?

SERVANT.   The dialect of your hometown.

MAN.   Bring them aboard and I'll speak to them. That may shorten our journey.

SERVANT.   As you wish.

The servant bows and exits. A moment later, he enters again in a mask and protective suit, ushering six women in. They are holding hands and walking unsteadily.

SERVANT.   Here they are. They're not well – they're blind.

MAN.   Go get some rest. Don't come back unless you hear me scream.

The man spreads a mat on the floor.

MAN.   Please sit. Tell me about the city of S———. Were you born blind or is this a result of the plague?

WOMAN 1.   Exalted sir, we are in this sorry state due to the plague, though we are delighted that our lives have been spared.

MAN.   From whence came the plague? When did it begin? Is it the fury of heaven? Does it come from the abnormality of man or the frenzy of animals? Tell me.

WOMAN 2.   Exalted sir, before satisfying your curiosity, may we have a drink of water? We have been adrift for ten days and are now as thirsty as the parched earth.

MAN.   Here is water, please help yourselves.
        There is fruit wine too, if you prefer.

WOMAN 3. A glass of wine can set free ten
        thousand thoughts. Exalted sir, your
        temples are broad and your jaw is
        square, your features tell us at a glance
        that you will live a long life. You must
        have many wives and concubines,
        an abundance of children and
        grandchildren. Might you have beef and
        vegetables to help the wine go down?
        We've hardly eaten anything for so long,
        in the gaps between our teeth there is
        only dust.

MAN.   Help yourself to anything on the table,
        no need to be polite. I live all alone
        without a wife. Gracious ladies, you are
        blind, so how could you know what my
        face looks like? Though in good health
        I am but skin and bones, and my face is
        long and narrow, not broad or square.
        Eat, eat your fill, then we'll talk.

WOMAN 4. Speaking of the plague, everyone could
        come up with their own reason for its
        existence. As the six of us drifted on the
        water, being unable to see, we could

only speak, and so we talked for ten
days, exhausting ourselves, but finally
we came up with an explanation we
could all agree on. Exalted sir, have
you a cigarette?

MAN.   Please don't stop, tell me the reason.
I don't smoke, my apologies.

WOMAN 4.   Three months ago, a fire started
one night and blazed till morning. It
spread quickly and burned down three
hundred wooden houses. That's five
hundred households, filled with over a
thousand poverty-stricken people. After
that, the plague arrived.

MAN.   Fire is extreme heat, but the plague
thrives in damp. How could one lead
to the other?

WOMAN 5.   This was no ordinary fire. After it
had died down, not a single corpse
remained, only smoke. Then a summer
rain fell, and even the smoke dispersed.
The streets were full of wandering
ghosts. Some hid in people's hair, some
rode their necks, some lurked in the
whites of their eyes or their mouths,
some concealed themselves in trouser

pockets. The six of us had gathered
in the countryside to sing when, all at
the same moment, we felt something
entering our eyes. There was a scraping
noise, as if a nail had pierced our
eyeballs, a stabbing pain, and then we
were blind.

MAN. What started the fire? Does anyone
know?

WOMAN 6. I do. Apparently a father flogged his son
for something he might not have done.
That night, the son set his father alight,
but the wind caught the flames and they
killed the son as well, then they spread
to the rest of the street and there was no
taking them back.

WOMAN 1. Very vivid, I feel like I'm seeing it, but
I heard different.

MAN. Go on.

WOMAN 1. Word on the street is a dragon turned
itself into a snake and hid among
the rafters of a house, waiting for a
thunderous night when it would be able
to fly back up to the sky. But a drunkard
spotted it and trapped it in a bottle of
alcohol. Months later, when the snake

was dead, the drunkard drank the liquor it had been steeping in. All of a sudden a fireball exploded from his belly, and the neighbourhood was set alight.

WOMAN 2. Word on the street is not to be trusted. I was nearby when the fire started, and fetched water to help put it out. No one knows better than me how it started.

MAN. Go on.

WOMAN 2. There was a boy of fifteen who lost his parents – he left to study abroad and soon rose through the ranks of the imperial court. He forgot he had a sister, and though she yearned in vain for his return, she eventually starved to death and became a ghost, haunting their old home. Three months ago, she heard her brother – now sixty – was returning to their hometown to visit family. Overjoyed, she set off some firecrackers, but somehow the flames from the ghost world found their way to the realm of the living and started the fire.

WOMAN 3. Shameless, all of you! I was right next door when the fire started, I was lucky

	to escape with my life. Who could know more than I do?
MAN.	Go on.
WOMAN 3.	A poor scholar lived next door to me. Every day he would mutter that S——— had been abandoned by the heavens and disaster would eventually befall us. He pored over his books all day long, trying to find a solution. Then the day came when he dozed off and knocked over his oil lamp, which set his bedding alight. The fire spread from there.
MAN.	Is that all?
WOMAN 3.	Yes. Don't forget, each of us has a wandering spirit lodged in our eyes.

Pause.

MAN.	If I were in S——— now, what would I see?
WOMAN 5.	An empty city.
WOMAN 6.	Some have fled by land, some by water.
WOMAN 1.	The rain has fallen steadily for months now.
WOMAN 2.	Gods and devils alike are gone.

WOMAN 3. Spirits wander the street bereft. They
sob all night long. Terrifying.

WOMAN 4. To leave is to die, to return is to live.

*The man stands and paces. The women turn their blind
eyes to him. He rings the bell.*

SERVANT. Master.

MAN. How much further to S———?

SERVANT. Another thirty li. At our present speed,
we should arrive tomorrow evening. We
have enough supplies should we need to
turn back.

Pause. The six women sing:

Oh the darkened sea, the whispering wind.
Devils roam the earth, hell is empty.
Divine fire burns forever our frail bodies.
The rain cannot extinguish your greed and
wrath.
Wanderer, you left home young and returned as
withered skin,
No longer recognized, tears streak your face.
In childhood when it snowed your mother
brought you soup,

Today your hair turns white and you have
>   nowhere to shelter.
You departed with a hopeful heart and return
>   like dust.
Who can be like the trees, forgetful of each era?
All that has passed is merely a prologue.
All that has passed is merely a prologue.

MAN.   Can our boat go any faster?
SERVANT.   Yes, we're the only craft on the water.
>   We could be there by morning.
MAN.   Raise all our sails and throw overboard
>   anything unneeded. Full speed ahead.

Before leaving S———, I visited my parents to tell
them my decision. They didn't try to dissuade me
– I was now unemployed, after all, and many of my
college classmates had stayed in Beijing, so we'd
be able to look out for each other. I gave my father
the crutch I'd bought him. It cost exactly as much
as I'd earned from my month on probation. My
mother handed me the address of distant relatives
in Beijing whom I could visit if I had the time. She
gave me the same address before I left for college,
but when I went there the family had moved away.

I said nothing and accepted the piece of paper; for all I knew, they might have moved back. The next day, I cleaned out my rented room and tossed the daffodils and roses in the trash. I phoned my landlord and said I was moving out tomorrow and didn't need a refund, even though the rent was paid up for the next month. He asked why I was suddenly leaving and I said I was going back to Beijing. What's so great about Beijing? he said. Once you start moving, you'll never be able to stop – next thing you'll be moving to New York, and then the moon. We chatted for a few minutes more before he remembered that we weren't actually friends and politely said goodbye. I bought a sleeper ticket for the following night. The next morning, without stopping for breakfast, I headed to Laodong Park. The singer was there again. I listened to her sing five songs and she seemed to remember me, nodding in recognition. I wanted to say something to her, but then decided not to. I sensed that she felt the same way. If I approached, she might leave. I napped on a park bench and wandered around all afternoon. There were many new roads in S———. I called a taxi, loaded my luggage into the trunk, and picked out places to visit on the GPS. After dark, I asked the driver to take me to Sitaizi. I could tell what had happened from some distance away, but I still insisted on driving right up close to make sure: the theatre was gone. Demolished. Nothing left but a trapezoidal mark in the ground. I didn't get out, just looked through the window. Where to next? asked the driver. The train station, I said. Did you know there used to be a two-storey building here? North or south station? said the driver. South station, I said. I'm heading home for dinner after this, said the driver. I haven't eaten a thing all fucking day.

Premonition

LI XIAOBING TELLS HIS WIFE THEY OUGHT TO sleep in separate beds. Confused, she demands a reason. He thinks about it: No reason, I just feel like sleeping on the sofa.

– Do I snore?

– No.

– Are you overheating? Am I too warm?

– No. You're always on the cool side and anyway we have air-con.

– Then why do you want to sleep apart?

Their son is already in bed. Daxing is seven, hyperactive and highly sensitive – even the slightest disagreement leaves a mark in his heart, and he's perpetually dredging up disputes from ages ago to prove that adults can't be trusted. At night, though, he sleeps with perfect calm and doesn't stir at all. I can't tell you why, says Xiaobing. No reason, all right? Can I go to sleep now? His wife is silent for a few seconds. All right, she says. I'll set up the sofa for you.

Fang Zhuo is a deputy director at the city's construction bureau. She's very capable outside the home and can keep talking coherently even after chugging a jin of baijiu. She stays on top of everything at home too, though there are a few issues. She's too fond of getting to the bottom of everything, for instance. Her catchphrase, *Give me a reason*, strikes fear into Xiaobing's heart. Whenever Fang Zhuo utters these words, his mind goes blank. Many things in life have perfectly good reasons that lose their shine when you say them out loud, like cut apples oxidizing. On this night, Fang Zhuo doesn't push Xiaobing because she understands him. He's a man of few words – he doesn't like to ask for anything. He'll wear the same clothes for three years in a row and isn't picky about his food – he'll eat anything that isn't rancid. If he wants to sleep alone, there's probably some logic behind it. It's late now; if she insists on finding out the reason, neither of them will get any shut-eye, and she has to be up early tomorrow for a work trip with her bosses. She puts bedding on the sofa, leaves a glass of water on the coffee table and retires to the bedroom.

Xiaobing lies on the sofa reading. He's not sleepy

at all. The living room is very quiet, the doors and windows are shut tight, and all the furniture is in its rightful place. He sits on the toilet for a while and emerges feeling a little drowsy. He turns off the lights, stretches out on the sofa and closes both his eyes and the book. Still sleep refuses to come. The reason he speaks so little isn't that he has nothing to say, it's because he prefers to save his words for the page. He's a science fiction writer, and not a bad one either. No, that's too modest. He's one of the finest science fiction writers working in Chinese, but he lives in the tiny city of S———, far from literary circles, so he isn't particularly famous. Besides, he's too reserved to care about getting his name out there. So what if a few strangers know who he is? It's not like they're dogs he can summon. Despite being an introvert, he's wildly ambitious, and his main aim is to bring down every other science fiction writer currently working. This leaves him a little isolated, but it also protects him. Raise your glass to the moon and your shadow makes a third. Those last two thoughts are related: the ambitious always need to amuse themselves, because talent is their only friend.

Around eleven at night on 8 August 2018, the science fiction author Li Xiaobing struggles to enter the realm of sleep. He tries shifting his posture, with or without a pillow, but nothing helps. S——— is a northern city of seven hundred thousand people. Used to be more, but the youngsters all left. You rarely see babies in the streets now. There are always a few unbearably hot days at midsummer, as if to shake a fist at the long winter and show that all four seasons are important. It rains on every one of those scorching days, but never for long enough to cool things down. All the rain does is increase the humidity so you really feel the heat.

Let's talk about why Xiaobing wants to sleep alone. He *does* have a reason: he woke up this morning with a premonition. He's lived with Fang Zhuo for eight years and with Daxing for seven, but this is something he wants to face alone. The premonition wasn't super clear, but that's the thing about premonitions. In his thirty-five years, he's experienced three of them. The first came the winter when he was five, lying on the kang with a fever. They lived in the suburbs back then. His parents both had to work, and the old lady who was taking care of him had set up a stall in the vacant lot outside their home, from where she did a thriving trade in tanghulu, candied fruit on sticks. In his dazed state, he suddenly felt that something was coming towards him, not walking or running, but flying. He wanted to tell the old woman about the feeling, but his mouth was welded shut. Thinking he was asleep, she snuck a cookie from the kang cabinet – a round yellow cookie from the metal tin that also held fruit leather. It was a little dry, so she reached for the water bottle on the sideboard. He opened his mouth to say the bottle wasn't in a good place, it was like a magnet, like a worm wriggling on a fishhook, like a well-fed antelope. At this moment, a bullet came through the window and hit the water bottle, which exploded with a gasp of relief. Glass shards scattered like sparks, embedding themselves in the old woman's face. No one ever found out where the bullet came from and no one stepped forward to claim it, not that they could have because it flew out another window, and who knows where it went or who it hit next. Xiaobing was the only person who saw the bullet, so surely the bottle had exploded on its own after all – perhaps the old woman's hands were too warm, or perhaps there'd already been hairline cracks no one had noticed. Xiaobing felt guilty anyway. If he hadn't been such a small child, he could have walked over and moved the bottle or the old lady.

The second premonition came when he was twelve. He'd just graduated from elementary school and his grandfather had recently died, although he didn't yet know how to feel grief. He'd rarely seen or spoken to his yeye, who'd taken to his bed when Xiaobing was eight and stopped talking. On the day of the funeral Xiaobing kept staring at his cousin, who was a year younger than him but already taller, dressed in buckled sandals that showed her red toenails. A well-put-together young woman. He wanted very much to play with her, but the atmosphere was too solemn for them to chase each other around. Yeye's children were huddled around the coffin weeping and howling, except for Xiaobing's father, who was like steel, completely expressionless, waiting for his siblings to finish crying so they could continue with the rituals. Out of nowhere, Xiaobing sensed something approaching the wake in search of Yeye. He wrenched his eyes from his cousin's ankles and turned to the doorway. Yeye fought in the War to Support Korea Against the USA. Could this be one of his brothers-in-arms? Or an enemy? Or perhaps he'd had a son while he was there that no one knew about, and this Korean-speaking man had tracked him down? Or was it the wandering spirit of some young person who'd died at his hand? A plump yellow dragonfly flitted in, darting this way and that before gently alighting on Yeye's cheek as if it had something to tell him. Yeye was unmoved, but as the dragonfly kept speaking, Yeye's ears and the corner of his mouth twitched. Startled, Xiaobing turned to look at his mother, who seemed drowsy from having woken up early. The howling was quieting down, and people were lowering their raised arms, when Yeye's corpse tumbled from the bier and landed face down. Everyone shrieked and rushed to lift him back up. The dragonfly took off again. Yeye looked different now. His jaw had slackened, revealing the fake ingot in his mouth. Xiaobing could tell Yeye had said what he'd wanted to say, confessed what he'd wanted to confess, because his face was no longer tight with tension. Just like that, he lost interest in his cousin's feet. People live such a very long time, and need to contain so many things, which requires enormous effort, yet death happens in just an instant and ends this lengthy existence with all its loves and attachments. A wave of sleepiness overtook him and he drifted off in his mother's arms.

The third premonition came when he was writing his first story. He was still working at the airplane factory in the city back then, researching the mechanics of wings. They'd had a meeting earlier that day, and now people were going off to play ping-pong, to shower or to pick up their kids from school. Xiaobing sat at his computer, seized by the urge to write something. Most of his twenty-seven years on earth had been spent in the realm of science: he'd studied math in college, and now his research mostly concerned physics. It had never crossed his mind to write anything. Even composing a simple note took him forever, and sometimes he'd miss out the subject, verb or object. He'd read *A Brief History of Time* and had heard of *Madame Bovary*, although he thought the author was Maupassant. The only Chinese author he knew was Lu Xun, because when he was a child the only books at home were Lu Xun's collected works, a set of small volumes with the author's face imprinted on them. He'd enjoyed Lu Xun's essays and letters, the former for their rigorous logic, and also – perhaps because Lu Xun had studied medicine – for the forensic accuracy of his insults, and the latter because Lu Xun was as scrupulously earnest as his headshot suggested, yet also managed to be romantic when needed, all of which demonstrates Xiaobing's contrarianism: he's never liked reading the mainstream pieces that everyone knows, but rather prefers uneven minor works. For some reason, that day at the factory he abruptly felt the sluggish river of time flowing before him, and in its glimmering ripples he saw his ageing face. A black hole opened in his heart, sucking every speck of light into roaring, meaningless dark. He created a new document, wanting to write a letter, but he only got as far as 'Dear' before getting stuck. He had no one to write a letter to. He tried very hard to think of people who lived elsewhere, but not one of them deserved a letter. Besides, letters ought to be on paper. Who wrote letters on a computer? Was this actually an official notification? An email? He deleted 'Dear' and typed 'I'. I what? He had no idea. Why begin with himself? What came after 'I'? What would he do? What kind of history did 'I', the subject, have? Was 'I' going to solve his own problems? Would 'I' break new ground or end up filled with regret? After more thought, he deleted 'I' and replaced it with 'he'. Now he felt as if he were floating overhead, finally able to see the smoke from Mama's cooking, the scent of their bedding. *He*. Here, let's have a hand gently shake him awake, that's right – he opens his eyes and finds himself at the bottom of the ocean drinking milk through a straw. Gravity? Pressure? They have no power down here. And now a complicated premonition struck Xiaobing. Unlike the previous two, this one was hybrid, formed of two opposing premonitions, like someone pulling apart hands clasped in prayer. He sensed that his life was going to change but he kept typing, the river of narrative surging ahead, an underground stream that an earthquake was now bringing to the surface, the roar of the water shattering his life, all phoniness cast aside, no longer worth noticing. At the same time another premonition told him something was about to fall, a descent more solemn than the flying objects he'd foreseen before. This was the final, climactic note of an opera before the curtain fell. A few minutes later, there came a scream from outside and the sound of frenzied footsteps. A test plane had crashed to earth and broken apart.

Now Xiaobing sits in the dark, suspicious of himself. He had this latest premonition at dawn, but it's been a full day and nothing has happened. He brought his son to English class and watched him on the security camera playing happily with the teacher (so far the only English word he's ever heard his son say is *no*). Then the boy had a nap while Xiaobing wrote in the study. He's been working on a short novel for six months or so. He's scrapped most of what he's written so far, but he's used to that: writers are people who find writing difficult. He accepts that he is changing, and will write a little each day, feeling neither joy nor sorrow. He knows there is a lot in his heart still, that there are many roads he will walk down, but the issue is that all these things are hidden deep down, and he will need to drill through many more layers of rock to get at them. He once thought of writing as a routine activity, like teeth cleaning, but now it feels more like pulling teeth.

Dinner wasn't too bad: he'd had two bowls of cold-water noodles. An old colleague asked him to go fishing but he declined because the weather report said rain. Next to writing, fishing is what he enjoys most. He and his buddies often go to the river that runs through S———, sometimes clear and sometimes murky. They prefer the upper reaches, where they catch tiny carp and release them again, very Sisyphean. Earlier tonight, his colleague messaged with a dropped pin: he'd found a place about an hour's drive away on the outskirts of S———, a brand-new lake, probably the result of abundant rain that summer or flood discharge upstream. Xiaobing was exhilarated – if river fishing was eating at a cafeteria, a small lake that no one knew about was more like the officers' mess. But he'd been uneasy all day and it was going to rain, so he put it off – it wasn't as if the lake would dry up in a single day.

Now his sleepiness and the premonition have both vanished without a trace. He glances at his watch: 11.50. He texts his former colleague, *Night fishing?* He waits twenty minutes. No response. The guy is still employed at their old workplace and has probably gone to bed – he has work the next day. For Xiaobing time is an open bank account whose funds he can allocate as he pleases. He texts another fishing friend: *New lake outside town, check it out?* His friend texts back that his father fell over while shitting and hit his tailbone, so he is now at the hospital taking care of him. No fishing lines for him, only IV lines. Xiaobing gives up and tries lying in the other direction, head where his feet were before. He manages to doze for half an hour, then he gets off the sofa, grabs his fishing gear, a raincoat and a flashlight, and heads out the door. He takes the elevator to the basement, gets in his car and drives off.

There isn't much traffic – the city is quiet at night, like a completely bald head. Dark clouds gather overhead, and the outdoor stalls that line the street by day have been stowed away. Xiaobing heads south. Once he gets past the new development zone, buildings grow sparse. The GPS leads him down a dirt track, past farms and rustic shacks, as if going south has also taken him back in time. Half an hour later, he passes a run-down hot-springs resort and sees a narrow hill. Are there still places like this so close to the city? He's lived here over thirty years and has never seen anything like this. He slows down for a closer look. The hill must be at least two hundred metres high, all alone in the landscape, tall and thin as a pagoda. It's too dark to see if there's vegetation on its slopes. How could such a thing exist? He runs through the physics and decides it's possible: perhaps a mountain was blasted to quarry rock, and this thin sliver is all that remains, a face with its jowls lopped off.

The road past the hill is full of potholes. The lake, when he comes upon it, isn't little at all – perhaps two thousand square feet. When his headlights sweep across the water it seems as solid as the pupil of an eye. The hill blocks it off from the road – he would never have found it if his friend hadn't sent him the specific location. He's the only one here now. One person, one car, one pair of headlights. Suddenly he feels a bit devilish, roaming the countryside rather than being tucked up in bed. His premonition from yesterday has completely evaporated and seems ridiculous to him now, mere early-morning grouchiness. Since he's here, he ought to go through with it and bring a couple of fish home, otherwise this story will seem even weirder when he tells Fang Zhuo tomorrow. Better to get some mud on his shoes, a bit of evidence. He parks, leaving the headlights on, grabs his fishing gear and heads to the lake. He's afraid of water and can't swim, so he'd never get into a boat, but he enjoys fishing. How to explain it? Getting in the water means entrusting yourself to it, while fishing is just a conversation, which he much prefers. The night wind is full of moisture. He unfolds his camping stool and sits on the shore.

No one will see Xiaobing on this night. He's in a hidden corner, off a road that rarely has any traffic at the best of times. He feels like a child playing hide-and-seek who's chanced upon the perfect spot that no one else will ever discover. He's been night fishing before, but never into the small hours of the morning. Fish need to sleep too, don't they? It seems a bit cruel to drive a hook into their cheeks as they're peacefully dreaming and yank them from the water. He feels contented as he settles onto his stool, even though mosquitoes are clustering around his ankles. The air remains muggy, even hotter than it was during the day. Nonetheless, the surroundings are quiet and the water doesn't stink at all – in fact it has a faint fresh fragrance.

Sometimes Xiaobing digs up one of his childhood photos and compares the way he looked as a kid to his son, who is growing to resemble him more and more. Daxing is taller than he was at the same age, but their features are remarkably similar, especially when he's upset – he frowns but never cries, as if he's concealing a grim smile, like someone trying to recreate their performance for a play revival. This sometimes delights Xiaobing, because it shows they're related by blood, and sometimes it terrifies him – was I really like that as a kid? How did I get to be the person I am now? What complicated process produced this thing, this present self? Xiaobing hardly ever goes to weddings but he loves attending funerals. With a white flower pinned to his chest, he observes the corpse lying there with no one to rely on any longer but itself, and thinks that the most joyous gatherings are nothing more than flowers that will one day wither and fall, leaving a bare branch. His face takes on the look of someone concealing a grim smile. And yet he hasn't given up on the world – the fact that he writes every day is proof of this. Even the most desultory writing is a conscious act, a rejection of simply going with the flow. In the winter he visits a second-hand bookshop, where he watches two young cashiers warming themselves by the stove. The shop is cold and dilapidated and has had to shift premises several times. Each time it moves they hire two new cashiers, and people always take the job. Only the stove remains the same. It hits him that one day, when he is old, he might work there instead of going into a home. He's good with his hands – he used to repair airplanes. As long as no one looks down on him for being elderly, he'll be fine.

The clouds have lowered and the wind is picking up. Xiaobing catches a fish, a healthy black carp, so plump it looks fake. He drops it into the bucket, where it quickly acclimatizes and starts swimming around. Xiaobing watches the fish, feeling pretty good. This is an achievement, a far bigger fish than you'd catch in the river. But then, abruptly, panic settles over him, sweat beads on his forehead, and his legs tremble in time to some unknown beat, as if he's being electrocuted. Lightning flashes for a few seconds in the distance, then thunder rumbles and blasts open the sky, beginning the deluge. Plump drops of rain coalesce into a downpour. Xiaobing hastily pulls on his raincoat. His first instinct is to run for the car, but he notices that his line has gone taut. Gritting his teeth, he tries to reel in, but his fishing rod gets dragged into the lake and his feet slip out from underneath him. From the lake emerges a man, hook stuck in his ear. The man yanks the hook out and hurls it back into the water, then unfurls a large umbrella and walks ashore.

Xiaobing is too terrified to move, or even to grab the screwdriver, his only weapon, from his trunk. The man walks up to Xiaobing and says, You're the fisherman?

– Yes.

– Don't worry, I just got here too. How many have you caught?

– One.

The man is dressed in a black suit, white shirt and leather shoes. If he wasn't a little too old – early forties – he could be someone's best man.

– Have you been waiting long for me?

– I wasn't waiting for you. I was fishing.

– Fishing in a place like this in the middle of the night? Why would you do that unless you were waiting for me?

The man is getting worked up, which makes Xiaobing fifty per cent more terrified. His clothes are bone dry despite having just emerged from the water, and he's . . . chewing gum?

– I'm just fishing to pass the time. I couldn't sleep.

– I've come a long way to be here. Could you please not look so anxious? We're just talking. Isn't it a good thing to meet a friend from afar? Or let's try another saying: there's no time like the present.

Or what about: how many times did we lock eyes in past lives before meeting in this one?

– Those are great sayings, but they have nothing to do with me. I should go, I have work tomorrow.

– Aren't you going to ask where I came from? Isn't curiosity the driver of human evolution?

Xiaobing is growing impatient. This guy has absorbed way too much government propaganda – he's even more of a nag than Fang Zhuo. Next thing you know, he'll be saying *Give me a reason*.

– Fine, where did you come from?

– An excellent question. I'm from a planet a million light years away. See how shiny the lake is? That's actually a flying saucer your hook has been rattling around in. I've given myself the name Andrew. What do you think?

– Sounds like an ordinary name.

– That's right. It's easiest to use an ordinary name. You're called Li Xiaobing, that's pretty normal too, and you're doing fine, so why judge a book by its cover?

Xiaobing has nothing to say to that. This guy is a little too fond of deploying proverbs. That head you've got on your shoulders is basically a display screen, says the man. I can tell that you're tense because your brain cells are twitching like crazy, and your heart is pumping more blood into your head, filling your veins to capacity. It's no use, you're not going to figure this out. I'm not intellectually superior or anything but you're definitely dumber than me. That's just the truth. Xiaobing is the equable sort and rarely gets into arguments, but he also has a strong sense of self-respect and always pushes back when insulted. Can you prove that I'm stupider? he says.

– I'm here to kill you. You didn't realize that, did you?

– How do you know I didn't?

–You haven't shown any sign.

– Why should I let you know how I'm feeling? Who do you think you are?

The rain is lighter now, and the dark clouds are melting away, leaving the night sky translucent. The two men stand by the hill on the edge of the lake, completely motionless. The carp flops around in the bucket, expending all its energy, but no one knows what it wants. Xiaobing is in trouble, but still he feels a little glee. He'd wondered as he lay on the sofa if he'd lost the ability to have premonitions – perhaps the three previous ones were just coincidences, or maybe he'd imagined them after the fact to make himself feel special. Now it seems he has no cause for worry. It might have taken a while for yesterday's premonition to manifest, but here it is. The only thing is, this time *he's* the water bottle.

Andrew closes his umbrella and hurls it into the lake, where it quickly sinks. He reaches into the water and pulls out a red telephone whose cord stretches into the depths. He leaves the phone by his feet, dries his hands on his trousers and says, You're still standing here even though you know I've come to kill you, so I believe you've accepted your fate.

– Not necessarily.

– Let me put it this way. Not only are you going to die, so are all seven hundred thousand people in S———. You're probably going to ask why, so I'll tell you: one among you has sinned.

– Obviously. Who among us has never done anything wrong?

– This is no ordinary sin. Someone here has done the unforgivable and stolen from us.

– How could we do that? You're high above us, looking down on the tops of our heads. What could we possibly take from you?

He's remarkably lucid for this time of night, and much as he hates speaking, he's proving to be a capable debater. Even as he admires his own per-formance at this crucial moment, in the gaps between speech he starts to think perhaps he actually is going to die, perhaps Andrew will kill him as he's threatening to. He doesn't feel much of anything, which surprises him. His body is like the water bottle, cool and slippery. If a doctor gave him a check-up now, he'd probably turn out to be healthier at this moment than ever before.

– Of course you couldn't take anything from us. We lost it while we were passing through S———.

– Hang on. If you lost it, you can't say we stole it.

– We did lose this thing, but you people haven't given it back, which means you stole it.

– How would we know who it belonged to? You just showed up. Look at you. How would we know this thing belonged to you? And even if we did, how would we find you? Did you put up a missing poster? Take out a radio ad? Go door to door? Were you even the person who lost this thing? Did it fall out of *your* pocket?

Andrew hesitates for a moment.

– It was an ancestor, but this thing belongs to my family. Does it matter who lost it?

– When my yeye was alive, he was always talking about our family treasures. Porcelain from the imperial palace. Rare *The Whole Country is Red* postage stamps. We lost them all when he had to flee during the war. Doesn't every family have imaginary valuables like this? Can you be sure this thing even exists?

Andrew sighs: Don't worry about that, it definitely exists. Not just in my grandfather's time but in his grandfather's too.

– What is it?

– A sentence.

– What?

– Yes, a sentence. My grandfather's grandfather was passing through this place when he thought of a particularly fine sentence. He couldn't hold it in, so he said it to someone from S——— who was drawing water from a well. S——— wasn't a city back then, of course, it was a village of ten households. The person he spoke the sentence to put their bucket on their shoulder and walked away, and my great-great-grandfather could no longer call the sentence to mind. It was lost. Generations of us have searched for it. For decades we've been asking the people who live here about it, but there's no sign. You must have hidden it.

– You can't remember?

– No. Ever since it left my ancestor's lips, it's passed from our minds.

– Then even if I returned it to you, you wouldn't recognize it.

– Not true. Imagine your son gets kidnapped and you don't see him again till he's seventy and you're a hundred. You'd still know right away that he was yours, wouldn't you?

– And you're going to kill us because of this lost sentence?

– Yes. Didn't your Lu Xun write about wanting to shoulder the gate of darkness to spare those who come after? That's what we did for you, but then you people forgot about us. Don't you think that means you deserve to die?

– But you're all right, aren't you?

– Not at all. We're finished. I'll tell you the truth: I'm the only one from my planet who's left. Did you sleep alone tonight?

– Yes.

– How would you like it if you were forced to sleep alone every night? I'm so lonely, I might as well be dead. I'm going to exterminate you people before I die. That will make me feel a little better.

– What's with the phone? If you're all alone, why do you have a phone?

– It's connected to a machine, not a person. Look up – the clouds have cleared. You see that star up there? I'm going to tell it to send ten times as much rain as now, and drown all you ingrates.

– Honestly, I don't believe you.

Andrew bends and dials a number. Hello, he says. Three minutes of rain, please. Apocalyptic. Five metres radius is fine. The star twinkles, dark clouds roll in and a column of rain begins falling precisely where Andrew and Xiaobing are standing. The car remains dry but the two of them look like they've just been dredged from a river. It's an old machine, says Andrew. It can only do rain, otherwise I'd have better options: earthquake, plague, fire, or I could just fling you all into outer space. Xiaobing goes over to his car, gets a towel to dry his face and offers it to Andrew.

– Any clues about the missing sentence? How many words is it, for instance?

– Five.

– Including punctuation?

– No.

– Maybe it's a saying. It's darkest before the dawn, for instance. Could that be it?

– No.

– Any other clues?

– Three nouns and a verb.

The night is an unlit house. Tired from standing, Xiaobing sits on the stool, and Andrew perches on a nearby rock. May I fish? says Xiaobing. It helps me to think. Go ahead, says Andrew. Want to catch a shark? No thanks, says Xiaobing. A carp is fine. Go ahead, says Andrew. Xiaobing baits his hook and tosses it into the lake. Three nouns and a verb. Probably noun–verb–noun–noun. *Xiaobing catches a gold leopard.* Although maybe 'gold' would count as an adjective in this case. What a needle in a haystack. Xiaobing thinks of Fang Zhuo and Daxing, sound asleep and dreaming of an imminent business trip (her) and cartoons (him), unaware they're about to get swept away by a flood. If only there were other clues. It's not Andrew's fault, he just happens to be the last person left from his planet and has held on to an ancestral grudge. On the verge of death, he's come here in his ratty old spaceship in search of some kind of justice. After all, don't we want back what was stolen from us by the invading Eight-Nation Alliance? Xiaobing understands how Andrew feels. A person about to die might well start thinking about what he's owed.

Andrew sits on the rock. Looking closely, Xiaobing can see his hair is going white at the temples, and his clothes are none too clean. The rain hasn't helped – they're ruined, like a cake past its expiration date. Maybe Xiaobing should have stabbed him with the screwdriver after all, but then if

Andrew can walk out of a lake of water, he probably can't be killed that easily. Turns out every planet has suffering people. Andrew has been pretty voluble since he emerged from the lake – probably he's been holding all this in for some time. The night sky glitters with stars, each of them secretly planning devastation. Who knew he'd been up there all this time?

The first story Xiaobing ever wrote was about water. Now he's met a man who walked out of the water, and S———— is about to be engulfed by water. Xiaobing has always been afraid of water, but that's how it goes, we end up encountering what we fear most. Andrew, says Xiaobing. Andrew's head jerks upright – he was asleep.

– What do you do? I mean, apart from drowning us all, do you have a job?

– I'm a postman.

– Do you people still need postmen?

– We do. We write letters and mail them every day. That practice has never changed. It's a hereditary position – my grandfather's grandfather was a postman too. His trip here was a perk of the job. That's why we're so sensitive to language. Losing a sentence is like losing a letter. My dad killed himself because he lost a letter, but that's another story.

One hour till dawn. If you don't come up with the sentence by then I'm making that phone call.

– Why should I believe you? For all I know, you could be a serial killer on the run.

Andrew's face turns bright red and he pulls out an envelope.

– This is the last letter I ever picked up. The sender and recipient are both dead.

– Can I see it?

– No way. Postmen never read the mail, that's a rule of the trade. Not even if both parties are dead.

– Think about it. You're the last person left from your planet. If you don't read it, then this letter might as well never have existed. I'm sure the sender wouldn't want that. Also – this is written in your language. It's someone talking to you. Didn't you say you were lonely? Wouldn't it feel good to have someone talk to you?

From the moment Andrew produced this letter, Xiaobing knew he would open it. That wasn't a premonition, just empathy. Of course, he might have already opened it dozens of times, he might know its contents by heart. They chat a little longer about their respective local customs, and when the conversation returns to the letter Andrew rips it open. I don't know your language, says Xiaobing.

Why don't you decide if you want to read it to me. Andrew thinks about this. All right, he says, but you can't tell anyone what it says, not even your wife. Go ahead, says Xiaobing. There are plenty of things I don't tell her.

My dear I,

Our unit has been defeated. The generals are plotting a counter-attack but all of us, down to the fleas on our bodies, know the situation is hopeless. As a consolation, our allegedly victorious enemies are rotting from the inside. Having fought them, we can sense this. They cannot be bothered to collect their dead, so the corpses fester in the heat of the battlefield. A plague is sweeping across us, not the sort that leaves boils on the skin, but one of despair in the heart. We know we will never return home. We will die in this place in a matter of days, in the most humiliating manner: we have been forced beyond the hills to the bank of the Styx and, lacking the strength to fight back, we will be massacred like mosquitoes. Suicides have risen massively in the last few days. The bodies are hung aloft as a deterrent to others, but the generals say even though these people will not become constellations after death, a full third of our troop has chosen to end their lives. I will fight to the

last, not from bravery but because I wish to witness
everything. Having come this far, I want to see how it
all ends. I hear that my hometown has been destroyed
and the very land torn up in battle. I have no idea if
you are still alive, it's been so long since you wrote. We
quarrelled when we parted, I think because I didn't
sit by your side during that final meal, but drank
so much that I forgot you existed, and at dawn the
next day had to be carried to the army transport.
My dearest I, if you are dead, I trust you thought of
me in your final moments. Barring the unexpected
I will be dead within three days, and although I did
not get the chance to marry you, I too will think of
you in my final moments. What we have is not mere
love, it's an encapsulation of all that is beautiful in
relationships. We are the world's left and right hand,
the river and its bed. We are a word consisting of two
letters. We are ordinary people, so no one knows the
power of our love. Like every indescribable secret,
no one knows of its existence, and no one will feel
sorrow at its passing, no one but the two of us.
How marvellous.

I would write more but time is running out. The
cannon fire draws close. If only we can hold our
position on this hill through the night. If you receive
this letter, please treat it as a proposal, albeit a virtual

*one. No response is needed. Please remember this and
find a way to go on living. If you are dead then it
does not matter, it's enough that we were once together.
May we recognize each other when we meet again.
That shouldn't be difficult – I only exist this time
round because I met you. What I believe is someone
like you will continue to exist even in death. This is
all I have time for. The postman has been waiting
too long.*

Your beloved X

Andrew folds the letter, returns it to its envelope
and tucks it into his pocket. He has a good voice,
low and steady, very suitable for reading letters out
loud. There is a glimmer of daylight in the distance.
The two men sit for a while. Xiaobing is stirred by
what he has just heard. He still can't think of what
the lost sentence might be. Andrew abruptly says,
This is why postmen aren't supposed to read their
letters.

– Why?

– It makes them too heavy to bear.

– I see.

– You don't see. These soldiers wrote letters until
the very end, and I kept delivering them, but most
had to be returned because the recipients were dead.

– I see.

– You don't see. But anyway, please hand over the sentence. You have half an hour left.

– I can't. It vanished too long ago.

– Then we must find it together. Let's begin with the first noun.

Xiaobing looks around him. Nouns. He must have written tens of thousands of nouns in his time – he's invented nouns for fantastical creations, but they all now seem very far away. Out of nowhere he understands that his task is not to find this sentence but to write it.

He guesses: Carp?

– No.

– Hill?

– No.

– Hope?

Andrew ponders for a moment: Interesting, but no.

– God?

– No.

– Devil?

Andrew jumps to his feet: Yes!

– The devil?

– That's right. The devil. Please continue.

Xiaobing stands too, and trots over to the lake.

What is the devil doing? Riding something? Holding a weapon? He turns: The devil likes?

– No.

– The devil takes?

– No.

– The devil hates?

Andrew comes a couple of steps closer: Interesting, but no.

– The devil flees?

– No.

– The devil fears?

Andrew nods: That's it, the devil fears. The devil fears, the devil fears, that's right.

– But what does the devil fear? Two more nouns. Which one should we find?

– Up to you. You have fifteen minutes.

Xiaobing glances at the red telephone: The devil fears the phone?

– You aren't afraid of phones, and neither is the devil.

– The devil fears water?

– No. Fire and water are nothing to the devil.

– The devil fears daylight?

– No, you're thinking of vampires.

– What are you afraid of, Andrew?

– You're wasting time.

– Are we actually talking about *the* devil?

– That's not important. The main thing is you've found the subject of the sentence.

– That's progress. Could you postpone the phone call?

– No. Don't forget I'm a postman.

– The devil fears promises?

– Warmer.

– The devil fears faith?

– Colder.

– The devil fears belief. Does belief count as a noun?

– You keep coming up with synonyms.

– The devil fears existence?

– Warmer, but also completely wrong.

At this moment, Xiaobing feels a premonition stronger than ever before, even more powerful than the one yesterday morning. That was but a pile of rubble – this is pure light beaming directly in his face, illuminating his swirling thoughts, the particles of light mingling with the particles of his mind until they are indistinguishable. A pronoun! Pronouns are nouns too. Warmer, yet further away. A bullet hitting a water bottle, a crashing airplane, a storm about to engulf this city, a missing sentence, a stubborn postman from far away, a letter with no recipient.

What I believe is someone like you will continue to exist even in death.

The devil fears his nonexistence, says Xiaobing.

Andrew looks like he wants to shake Xiaobing's hand, but slaps him on the shoulder instead. The sun is not fully up yet, but already its heat can be felt. The lake begins to evaporate like a garment shrinking in the wash, all the water returning to the sky. The cord shortens and the telephone tumbles into the lake. The hill next to them like an antenna folds neatly in two, forming a pair of crutches that walk *tak tak* into the centre of the lake, which is rapidly turning into a vast plain. The TV tower with its metal spike becomes visible in the distance. Andrew brushes his hair back, reaches into his pocket to make sure the letter is still there, tips the black carp from the bucket into the last of the water, then jumps in himself. A few minutes later, he and the lake have both vanished without a trace.

Sen

I.

HOU SEN EXAMINED YING QIANLI'S WOUND. The bullet had gone through his left ribcage and grazed his spine as it exited his back. He couldn't believe that even after getting shot, Ying Qianli had managed to run five hundred metres, break free of the crowd and clamber into his rickshaw, enduring the seven-minute ride back to the clinic. The bullet hadn't lodged in his body; as long as they could staunch the blood flow, his life shouldn't be in danger. Ying Qianli joked that he'd had to apologize for spattering several bystanders and reassure them that the blood would wash out with warm water. Then it seemed to hit him that he might die. His brow furrowed and he tried to come up with some last words. Lord, he said, actually . . . But before he could get any further, he fainted from blood loss. He was fine, though – of this, Sen was certain. Call it a doctor's instinct. Sitting alone in the clinic's front room, Sen thought: I'm sure he's all right for now.

Ying Qianli was an acquaintance from Hou Sen's time studying in England. His landlord's son, to be precise. The landlord was a British noble-man, or at least the descendant of noblemen, and a thoroughgoing Sinophile. His family bought Chinese silk and porcelain when it first arrived in England, liked what they saw, and acquired more and more. To start with, they'd made their pur-chases through a comprador, but that wasn't the most reliable method. You'd order a snuffbox and receive an opium pipe, or request a bowl from the court of the Qianlong Emperor, and instead he'd bring you a faded vase of uncertain provenance, still filled with withered petals. To circumvent this, they gave themselves Chinese names and began going to China themselves, and, even taking into account the risk of counterfeit goods, the inconvenience of travel, the difficulty of valuing their finds and the despair of being hoodwinked, there was simply no comparison to waiting at home for their purchases. They had discovered the joy of uncovering new treasures themselves. They first travelled to Shang-hai in 1842, and subsequently came every six years or so – in 1848, 1853, 1860 and so on, up until the Boxer Rebellion of 1900, which is also when Ying Qianli's grandfather fell gravely ill. There followed a gap of over a decade, until the grandfather died. The father began travelling to China himself with a couple of servants. He visited Lanzhou, Xi'an, Beiping, Jiaodong, and was robbed, cheated, detained by the army, and abandoned in the wilderness by a starving muleteer. When the older servant died, they buried him in Henan. After a valorous display in which he shot dead thirty-five bandits in Sichuan, the younger servant vanished without a trace, perhaps murdered in retaliation or perhaps simply losing heart and fleeing. None of these setbacks deterred the Ying family from continuing their Chinese expeditions, until Ying Qianli's father suffered a stroke in 1927 – coincidentally the year of the Nanchang uprising – which brought an abrupt end to the Chinese wanderings of this Catholic clan.

By the time Hou Sen arrived in England they were a family in decline, partly due to the patriarch's illness and partly because they had spent decades collecting artefacts and pursuing pleasure rather than managing their fortune. Ying Qianli was an only child, and his main interests were hunting and movies. After his father's death, he began selling off his possessions and roaming the world with the proceeds. So vast were the family's holdings that they sustained him until 1939. He was in a Japanese hotel when news arrived that Britain and Germany were at war, and he swiftly realized that he was no longer welcome. The Japanese friends who'd been carousing with him now boarded trains to the docks to join the war effort. One hanger-on, unable to ship out due to lung disease, tried to attack and rob Qianli while he was drunk. Qianli knocked him to the ground, left him a little cash, and sold the final jade amulet in his possession to buy passage on a boat. In Beijing, he threw himself on the mercy of Hou Sen.

Hou Sen was ten years older than Qianli, who really ought to have called him 'Uncle', but because Hou Sen had always called the older Ying 'Uncle', as an adult Qianli called him first 'Brother' and then simply Sen. Hou Sen was born in Fengtian. His father was a high-ranking officer under the warlord Zhang Zuolin, although he rarely set foot on the battlefield. His duties were mainly analysing military strategy and training the troops. When Sen was twenty-three, he was due to study railroad engineering in Berlin. The Fengtian army was badly in need of talented railroad engineers. Japanese trains were steadily blanketing the northeast, and Zhang Zuolin hoped to claim some territory for himself, at least around Fengtian and Liaoyang. Many times he expressed a wish to hear trains he'd manufactured rumbling down tracks he'd laid.

Then early one winter morning, Sen's father pushed the cadets he was training too far, causing one of them – a recent recruit from Chaoyang – to snap, wrest the gun from him and shoot him dead. The cadet ran back to his dorm and, before a picture of his mother, put the barrel in his mouth and pulled the trigger. Zhang Zuolin met with Sen personally to ask what his plans were. His voice was raspy, and though he'd seen more than his share of death, he remained humble as befitted a true leader. Sen replied that he had decided to study medicine instead of engineering. He no longer wished to set foot in Germany, since the Mauser pistol that had killed his father was German-made. At the time, Germany was under the control of the allies and would soon sign the Potsdam Agreement, but based on the Germans' prowess at manufacturing weapons, Sen felt they would be at war again soon enough. Zhang Zuolin granted his request. He remembered a prosperous Englishman he'd encountered while he was still a bandit; although they'd started off on the wrong foot, they soon become fast friends. Zhang Zuolin once sent the Englishman a crate of bird fossils and received in return a shipment of hand grenades made of chocolate, a typical British joke that the warlord found highly amusing. He dispatched Sen to London with a letter of introduction. Sen arrived to find the Englishman sick in bed, no longer so humorous. Not only did Sen have to fend for himself, he ended up having to take care of the Englishman's son, serving as both tutor and guardian. Studying medicine required a knowledge of Latin at this time, so Ying Qianli learned both Latin and Chinese from Sen, adopting Sen's northeastern accent. When he came of age, Ying Qianli made his first trip abroad, to Rome. Qianli's father had died by then, and Sen realized as Qianli left that he was feeling the melancholy a parent usually feels when their child first leaves home.

Two days after getting shot, Ying Qianli woke in the night and went into the study, where Sen was reading. He sat by the low table and made himself some tea. Sen put down the book and turned to look at him. He was wearing a white short-sleeved shirt (it was actually long-sleeved, but because Qianli's sleeves were permanently rolled up, Sen always thought of his shirts as short-sleeved), canvas trousers and Neiliansheng cloth shoes. Sen had had these items waiting for him. Qianli was 190 centimetres and broad-shouldered, and his clothes needed to be made to measure. It was November in Beijing, the leaves were yellowing on the trees, the full moon was high in the sky, and cold air tramped around the courtyard as if in heavy boots – yet Qianli wore his sleeves rolled up as always, so impervious to cold that the slightest movement raised a healthy sweat on his neck. Sen looked at him, legs curled under the table, teacup tiny in his vast hand, and frowned. How could he hide this giant? No matter where he went, he'd take up too much space. How do you feel? asked Sen. Wonderful, said Qianli. Did you know that when people fell ill in the eighteenth century, they were treated with bloodletting? Now I know how good it feels to lose some blood. It's like there's more space in my body, like air can pass through me.

Sen crossed the room to sit opposite Qianli. Even while studying western medicine in England, Sen had continued drinking Chinese tea. This tea set had been made specially for him. The resin in the gong dao cup left it resistant to heat, and it was marked with gradations for easy pouring. The teapot was apparently from Angkor Wat, and had been given to him by a patient, though he had insisted on paying market price for it. Now he refilled the teapot and rinsed Qianli's cup. As he poured more tea he said, Do you know that Japanese man?

– No. I saw his photo in the papers. It's a good likeness.

– Did someone order you to kill him?

– Am I a prisoner?

– No. You're safe for now. But if I can understand why you did what you did, it'll be better for both of us. Had you already planned this when you came to stay with me?

– No. I decided this morning when I saw him in the newspaper.

– Most people can read a newspaper without wanting to kill someone.

– That's true. That's because you only see the words, but I see more than that. This Japanese officer killed many people, most of them Chinese.

– Perhaps so.

– No perhaps about it. It's a fact. He beheaded a Chinese prisoner in Shanghai. She was a fan of his, and even as he chopped off her head she was calling out the names of his films.

– A fan?

– Yes. He was a director before the war, and shot

several sword-fighting epics. He was considered one of Japan's most promising young directors. I saw his movies while I was out there, he's pretty good. In one of them he cameos as a blind pipa-playing monk.

– You're British. What does any of this have to do with you? People get killed in wartime, that's what it means to fight a war. What do you expect?

– This isn't about the war. It's about me and him – I'm a fan of his too. His work deeply moved me. Then I heard on the Japanese news that he'd cut off a fan's head to intimidate other prisoners, and I began wishing he'd survive the war just so I could meet him. I didn't expect him to be here in Beijing. Seeing as it'll be hard to chop his head off, I'll just aim to kill him.

– Have you talked this over with your God?

– That's private. Now, are you going to help me or report me?

– Neither. I can't ask you to leave, because you won't survive long out there. So I'll go. I have friends in Shanghai I can stay with. I've left some money in the drawer in your room, along with a week's worth of anti-inflammatories. Let's say goodbye, I doubt we'll ever meet again.

Being unmarried, Sen only packed a small bundle.

But instead of going to Shanghai, he checked into a hotel two streets away. He understood young Master Ying well enough to know he wasn't lying. It was difficult to comprehend his enmity for the Japanese director, but Sen was sure Qianli wouldn't give up. He would try and fail again, and there was no way he'd survive a second attempt. When that happened, Sen could move back into his place and go on being a doctor. He stared at the lamp, not yet ready to sleep. He recalled his mother's premature passing, his father's accidental death, his own long journey to study medicine. After coming back to Beijing he'd opened a clinic, and now worked more than ten hours a day there. Two months ago, he was treating people practically for free in order to establish himself, then the foreigners and Beijing's upper crust began to show up. He was rigorous in his practice, and was particularly good with children – no matter how rowdy or pain-stricken they were, they turned quiet and biddable as soon as they stepped into his office. He had an instant rapport with them, perhaps because of the years he'd spent living with young Qianli – or maybe the kids pitied him because they recognized that he was an orphan.

Qianli's arrival a week ago had made Sen the happiest he'd been in years, though he'd known a day like this would come – ever since Qianli was a child, Sen had been his first port of call in times of trouble, and Qianli was destined to keep getting into trouble. Now they were both orphans far from home, but one was scrabbling to make a living while the other pursued pleasure. They talked about the past – how Mr Ying had died with a Chinese scroll painting clutched in his hand, or about the hunting expedition during which a teenaged Qianli had shot a reindeer in the shoulder, only to get closer and realize how beautiful she was. He'd half-expected her to start speaking human words in her desperation to survive. They brought her home and Sen successfully operated on her.

On this visit Sen bought Qianli a bicycle, and they rode along the hutongs together until they were tired, then went into a teahouse. Listening to cars crunching over fallen leaves outside, and to the crowds passing through the busy teahouse, Sen no longer felt alone. He thought about asking Qianli to help out at the clinic. But no, Qianli didn't really need to do anything, since Sen earned enough to support both of them. The Japanese generally didn't give doctors a hard time. He only had to keep the clinic going, and it would do better and better. Eventually a woman would love him. When that happened, Qianli could do as he liked. Sen might leave the clinic to a son, if he had one. He may not have generations of wealth to pass on as the Yings once did, but he had a skill that would prevent him from hitting the depths the Yings had now sunk to. A Japanese director? A Japanese director who came to join the war in China? Sen couldn't understand this. He didn't enjoy movies and had no interest in that sort of thing, because he had no time – he'd been busy for his entire thirty-something years on this earth – and because he didn't believe in fictional worlds. His work required him to worship at the altar of reality. A single vein was more meaningful than all the living people who'd ever pretended to be corpses on screen.

A month passed, and Sen was basically on vacation. Apart from eating, sleeping and going for walks, all he did was read the papers in search of news of Qianli – that he'd been shot dead or had been arrested – but there was nothing. He read that Yamamoto Shinji, the Japanese officer, suffered a light wound to his collarbone from the shooting but fully recovered. Yamamoto was reported attending a party for Beijing artists, where he performed an excerpt of Noh drama. Leisure was hard for Sen, and he lost weight from sleeping too much. Three days later, the newspapers reported that Yamamoto was being transferred from Beijing to the front line, although the article didn't say where exactly. Sen packed up and returned to the clinic. Qianli was gone. He'd taken all but two of the anti-inflammatories. The place had been carefully cleaned. No farewell note. Sen rested for a day, then started working again. No one came looking for Qianli, and he didn't return. Half a year later, Sen had a telephone installed, and bought a new tea set. Three months after that, he hired an assistant.

2.

AFTER I GRADUATED FROM MEDICAL SCHOOL IN 2013, I went against my parents' wishes and took an internship at the film archives. My main duties were categorizing film reels and managing our screening schedule. In July 2014 I was taken on full-time. At the start of 2015, I went with the archive director, Sun Heyang, to a conference in Japan. Director Sun suggested we try to visit some important figures in film who'd been active during the Shōwa era, including directors, screenwriters, actors, cinematographers and lighting designers. Most of them turned us down because their best days were long since past and we were nobodies, yet more pilgrims hoping to bask in their reflected glory. They were all ancient, and only a few were still capable of sustained conversation. Some lay in bed all day and were only lucid for short intervals, making interactions with their own families tricky, never mind with interviewers. The handful who agreed to see us were mostly represented by family members, and all wanted far too much money, given our limited budget. In the end, the only person we actually managed to meet was Yamamoto Shinji. He and his family accepted the fee we offered, and although he was ninety-eight, he was clear in his mind and strong in his body. Occasionally he still made a cameo appearance in a young person's film. In his free time he liked to ride his bike to the shops of Omotesandō. He sometimes forgot his PIN at the checkout, but give him a little time and he'd remember it, since it was written inside the hat he always wore. The shop assistants knew and would discreetly remind him.

We arrived at Yamamoto's home in the afternoon. He lived in a two-storey home at the intersection of Shibuya and Omotesandō, an oasis in a bustling district. A forty-five-year-old live-in housekeeper looked after him, while his business affairs were taken care of by his son, Yamamoto Hideo, and his daughter-in-law. Hideo was waiting for us at the front door, dressed in a black suit. The orchids and spider plants by his side had just been watered, and there among them was old Mr Yamamoto's bicycle, polished to a shine, gleaming so brightly you'd think it had been watered too. The old director was waiting for us in the living room. He wore a white shirt, black trousers and snow-white socks. In his shirt pocket was a black fountain pen. Both his watch and his wedding ring were gold. When he stood to greet us, he was easily over 180 centimetres. Given that people often shrink with age, I could imagine that back in the day he must have been exceptionally tall for a Japanese man. We shook hands and sat, and the housekeeper came in with tea and snacks. Director Sun was an expert in Japanese film and, having studied in Japan, he spoke the language well. I'd taken some Japanese modules at university, but although my reading and comprehension were okay, I found speaking difficult and would have struggled to discuss the minutiae of the industry. Instead, I took charge of recording the conversation and taking notes.

Director Sun politely praised the house and the tea, then launched into an explanation of why we were there. There was the interview, which we would publish in our organization's magazine and on other platforms, but we hoped too that Mr Yamamoto would be able to give us some films to screen in our building, for which we could offer him a portion of the box-office proceeds. Young Mr Yamamoto had anticipated our request and handed over a two-page list of his father's films, arranged chrono-logically and indicating where copies of each could be found. Some were held at studios or arts insti-tutes, others in archives like ours. Yamamoto Shinji pushed the pages aside, indicating that we should look at them later, and asked how we usually split the proceeds. Director Sun said our standard was fifty–fifty. Yamamoto said he wanted eighty per cent, sticking up his thumb and index finger to indicate *eight* in the Japanese way. That would be difficult, said Director Sun, given the cost of our venue and staff, not to mention taxes. Besides, this would be the first time Yamamoto's films would be screened in China, which surely had a significance beyond money. Director Sun hinted that previous screenings of Japanese films had also been on a fifty–fifty split, and this was now considered established practice. Yamamoto nodded and said, But I'm better than them. Director Sun smiled politely and said nothing.

I have an understanding with the Americans too, said Yamamoto. I'm greater than them. He closed his thumb and finger and said, Seventy. Director Sun glanced at me. Mr Yamamoto, he said, I personally like your films very much, which makes me a bit of an outlier, and so I'll be selfish and make an exception for you: sixty per cent. An odd expression flitted across Yamamoto's face, reluctance mixed with smugness. With an old man's bluntness he said, Fine, sixty, that's better than fifty anyway. Try the suncakes, a Taiwanese friend sent them to me. If you don't have some I could easily eat twenty myself. And let's have some sake too. The housekeeper waited for young Mr Yamamoto to nod his agreement before going to fetch three bottles of sake.

Yamamoto swiftly downed his bottle. I'm not much of a drinker, and medically speaking, alcohol is most harmful when taken in the afternoon, so I passed most of mine to him. He went on drinking, twisting the ring around his finger as if that was somehow increasing his enjoyment. Young Mr Yamamoto took his leave. He shook our hands very sincerely and said he hoped we'd visit again, then he instructed the housekeeper not to let his father eat or drink too much. He bowed deeply to Yamamoto, who pursed his lips and didn't so much as glance at his son. After a while Yamamoto said, Where have you come from? Beijing, said Director Sun. In autumn, leaves fall in Beijing, said Yamamoto. I wrote that in my journal. The city walls get in the way, but they're beautiful to look at. Hey, young man, you haven't said anything. Do you know Japanese? A little, I said. Beijinger? he asked. No, I'm from a small city in the northeast. But will you die in Beijing? he said. I thought about it, trying to remember the Japanese word for *choice*. What do you want to say? Director Sun asked. I'll translate. If I have a choice, I said, I won't die in Beijing. Director Sun passed this on. Yamamoto nodded. I see, I see. I almost died in Beijing. I was standing in a university sports field giving a speech when a bullet grazed my neck. The marksman was good but fired from quite far away. The bullet came from a left-handed Webley revolver – that's a British gun from the First World War. They're much less accurate at anything over fifty metres. The shooter was truly exceptional. Can I have more of your sake? Thanks very much. He got away and I survived, so you could say we both lost.

The setting sun came slantwise through the French windows, creeping towards us, dappling Yamamoto's legs. I'd seen a couple of his films while I was still at school, both from after the war. One was about a storyteller who summons the spirit of Tokugawa and becomes friends with him, but they have a falling out and he exorcises the ghost. All I could remember of the second one was a man kills his wife. Some of his films had major flaws, but they all contained an irresistible zest for life. He was truly an amazing artist.

We found the rickshaw driver who helped him get away, said Yamamoto. He said they didn't know each other and he had no idea this person had tried to assassinate me. My attacker was wearing a mask, so the driver didn't see his face, but from his body odour and accented Chinese, he thought he was probably a foreigner. We believed the driver but killed him anyway. He'd picked up the wrong customer and so bad luck settled like a crow on his head. Must have been an American spy. To think an insignificant official like myself had caught his eye – what unusual taste. For all I knew, he'd boarded a ship by then. Soon after I recovered, my unit was notified that we were being deployed. Two nights before our departure, I got a letter from the gunman apologizing for the assault and challenging me to a duel. In order to make up for the mistake caused by his past weakness, I could fire the first shot. The place would be the Seventeen-Arch Bridge at the Summer Palace, and the time would be ten the following night. I didn't tell my subordinates, but wrote a letter to my family detailing the various arrangements that would need to be made in the event of my death. If I survived, they could ignore the letter. The next day, I set out in civilian clothes. Are you taking notes? Yes, I said. What for? I don't know, I said, I thought you'd want me to take notes. I have a journal, he said. I can have a copy made for you if you like. I'm very aware that I won't live much longer, and I'd prefer if you'd look at me while I'm talking. I put away my notebook and he nodded his thanks.

I got to the bridge on time, he said. The man was already there. He was a good-looking westerner, even taller than me. Despite the Beijing winter he was dressed for summer: pure white shirt, sleeves rolled above his elbows, cloth shoes. We had no language in common, so I wasn't able to ask why he wanted to kill me. I never found out. Seeing him in person, I no longer thought he was a spy. By miming we managed to communicate that we both thought the Summer Palace was very beautiful. He'd strolled around before arriving at the bridge, and I'd visited when I first came to Beijing. Next, we established the rules of our duel. I would stand five arches from the southern end of the bridge, and he would do the same at the northern end. I would fire first. He was a very interesting person. I felt as if I were a teenager again and he was a playmate from my hometown. The two of you didn't live through the war so you won't understand this, but at that moment, it didn't make much difference to me whether I lived or died. That feeling has stayed with me a very long time.

My first shot missed, though it startled the birds in the nearby woods and the wild ducks paddling on the lake. I knew my death was approaching, and for a panicked moment I wondered if I should jump into the water. Then he tried to fire, but his antique gun jammed. He said something that sounded like an apology and looked down at his firearm. I ran up to him and fired again, but I was breathing so hard I only managed to hit him in the leg. I shot again, this time directly at his chest. He died very quickly, mouth agape, a rasping noise coming from his throat as if he was trying to say something. His final word was Shen. I didn't know what that meant. Shen. When I got back to Japan, I looked it up in your language and learned that it's the word for god. Shen. Why was he calling for his god in Chinese? I couldn't understand it. Do you have any idea?

Director Sun and I shook our heads. If he didn't understand after thinking about it all this time, what hope did we have?

I pushed the corpse into Kunming Lake, said Yamamoto. Later, I used this image in one of the films I guess you'll want to screen. I transplanted it, though – it's not set during the war. You know the one I mean? It made me famous in the West. I imagined Shen as a person, an old friend who was also an orphan. Maybe I was influenced by Dickens. Who knows? Anyway, that was my thinking. Now look, I'll end up finishing all of these suncakes if you don't have some. Won't you help me out?

Daughter

I DON'T NOTICE THE BOY AS I LEAVE THE BOOK-store. It's not until I've crossed two streets and am making my way down a busy sidewalk that he jumps out in front of me. I'm thinking about how I got Dostoevsky's time of death wrong earlier. I don't particularly rate Dostoevsky – Tolstoy's the writer I reread – yet at every event I somehow end up ram-bling about Dostoevsky while Tolstoy doesn't get a mention. There's so much to say about Dostoevsky: sentenced to death but reprieved at the last minute; faced every setback with superhuman resilience; in his old age found a woman who stuck by his side no matter what; forever talking to God; permanently in debt. Talking about Dostoevsky makes my life easier because I don't need to do much thinking – I can make use of other people's opinions, maybe draw from André Gide's lectures or one of the many scholars who came after him. If I were to speak about Tolstoy

I'd need to prepare, because Tolstoy lacks a distinctive style; I'd be a mouse trying to eat an elephant, not sure where to bite first. Dostoevsky is a small island with the expanse of the ocean protecting him, diluting him, confining him. I just have to set my boat free on those waters and time simply passes.

Beijing's sidewalks are a jungle. As soon as the lights change, cars swerve past one after another, then a stream of motorcycles, e-bikes and motorized wheelchairs, and pedestrians are caught midstream, trying not only to move forward but also simply to survive. The boy appears as I'm trying to remember when Dostoevsky actually died (November? No, February, a winter of endless snow. That's right, a pen holder fell to the ground and he was moving a walnut cabinet to get it when he had the brain haemorrhage. What kind of pen holder?), and a motorbike passes practically under my armpit.

Then the boy pops up and says: I have a question.

– Wait, have you been following me?

– Not for long. Only since the bookstore. You smoke Zhongnanhais, you spit a lot, and you walk with one shoulder higher than the other – that will ruin your shoes.

The lights are about to change so I forge ahead and he walks backwards as if he's a cart I'm pushing.

– What's your question? You could have asked it at the bookstore, I don't remember you raising your hand.

– I wasn't at the event, I waited for you outside. Everything you said in there was fake.

I stop and stare at him. Early twenties, about 175 centimetres, very skinny, longish ink-black hair straggling across his forehead. White tote bag with a picture of an accordion that, when I look closer, is actually a ribcage. White canvas shoes and, even though it's a chilly October, rolled-up trousers that reveal ankles thin as drumsticks.

– Go ahead, what's your question?

– How come you've done so many events and you've never once mentioned me?

– Why would I mention you?

– Because I'm a better writer than you.

– Wow. And what might your name be?

– You wouldn't know it.

A gust of wind rushes between us.

– If I may be frank, I've met many people like you – though of course you might actually be special and not a lunatic like the rest. Even so, you don't need me to prove you're such a great writer. Dostoevsky isn't great because someone else said so.

– It's Tolstoy you're imitating. Though very

shallowly. So listen, I'm not after your autograph, I'm not in some boring-ass book club, I'm not the sort of loser who goes to a bookstore and nurses a cup of coffee all evening just to get into the pants of some woman who's addled her brain with novels. I'm a better writer than you, and I hope you'll acknowledge that.

– Okay. What have you published?

– Nothing. I haven't written anything yet.

– Amazing. I need to get home for dinner, then I have work to do – as you said, I'm a writer. Why don't you go and write something that's better?

He produces a notebook from his bag and says, Agreed. Give me your email and I'll send it over when I'm done. Make sure you let me know if you agree I'm better. The notebook is crammed with words and drawings. I find a blank space where I write an email address I don't check often. Taking a closer look, I realize he has copied out *Heart of Darkness* in tiny handwriting, I'm not sure which translation.

The business intrusted to this fellow was the making of bricks – so I had been informed; but there wasn't a fragment of a brick anywhere in the station, and he had been there more than a year – waiting. It

seems he could not make bricks without something,
I don't know what – straw maybe. Anyway, it could
not be found there and as it was not likely to be sent
from Europe, it did not appear clear to me what he
was waiting for.

The pictures don't seem connected to the text – maybe they're based on ancient Greek or some mythology I haven't heard of: images like a two-headed woman and a dragon gazing tenderly at an infant. I hand him back the notebook and say, Why me? There are plenty more awesome writers out there, just have a look on Baidu.

– Who do you think is greater, Sherwood Anderson or Faulkner?

– Faulkner, I guess.

– But Anderson inspired Faulkner, and some things you wrote have inspired me, even though your writing isn't as good as mine. That's why I've come to you. Also, you have a literary column so you count as a critic, and I'd like you to write about my novel.

– You've thought of everything. See you around.

– Check your email. I'll send it by tomorrow morning.

I rush off because he's reminded me that my

column is due tomorrow, and unlike at a bookstore event, I can't just spout nonsense. That's what I like about being a columnist – the job forces me to think deeply rather than fob people off with the same clichéd phrases – though I suppose you could say columns are kind of fake too. Ahead of me, a homeless person sleeps by the side of the road with a thick blanket over him, his large dark head sporting a red boil, yellow leaves scattered over him as if someone has showered him with flowers. I place a one-yuan coin next to him and he doesn't stir. Maybe it's an electric blanket. I do walk awkwardly, I wrecked one of my ankles playing soccer as a child, and in order to hide it I limp with the other leg too, and so the sides of my shoes often drag along the ground. Oh, and I try to do a good deed whenever I get the urge to write something, though that's a tip I'll never share.

Downstairs from my place is a trendy supermarket selling the sort of food foreigners eat, although it's mostly locals who shop here. I buy two bottles of Korean milk, a box of American cookies and a 12-pack of German beer. As soon as I open my front door I smell cat shit. My cat is named Wu Song, after the tiger-killer. He's not really my cat, he was foisted on me by a friend who was leaving the country. I had a dog once, but I seldom leave the house, and after a month stuck inside he developed kennel cough. After he recovered I gave him to an outdoor running coach. Then a stray cat in my compound started following me around. She was plump, with glossy black fur, and I invited her to come live with me, but she had fleas that tormented me so much I had to chase her away again. Wu Song's name was originally Henry the Second. My friend bought him from a pet shop on a whim. He's four months old and looks like Garfield – ginger, large eyes, flat face. He sneezes a few dozen times a day and poops on my sofa no matter how many times I smack or spray him. I went online to look into the problem, and the most reliable answer was: your cat is an idiot. Thinking about his IQ, I realized that in all the time he'd been living with me I'd never heard him meow, not even when I smacked him. If I hit him too hard he grins and squeezes out another poo. So he's mute, but that's fine. We get on better because he's quiet.

I clean up the cat shit, top up his food bowl, brew myself some tea, open the cookies and start work on my column. Three hours and five cups of tea later, I've eaten all the cookies and failed to produce a single word.

To be honest I often feel lonely, but I'm happy

this way. For many years I longed to burrow into the mass of humanity and form intimate connections, but I couldn't change myself and nor could the world. It was like with my pets – I didn't want to go out so they developed a cough; they got fleas and I ended up annoyed. In the end we always part ways. Writing fiction is different. My characters might loathe me, they might find me hard to live with, but they're my creations and so they have to accept their fate. I create their universe, I provide the blood that flows through their veins and the hair that sprouts on their heads. When I offer up a world I've created, other people read it and imagine they've learned something about me, but they're probably way off base. They think reading my work brings us closer, but I'm the one who gets to determine the distance between us. Sure, this means I end up living like a prisoner, but everything has a price, and no matter what, your life is going to get used up. That's probably what Schopenhauer meant when he said we live to keep from dying, we walk to keep from falling over.

I smoke a few more cigarettes and think about the boy from earlier this evening. The world is full of self-important people, some cute and some annoying. This boy isn't one of the annoying ones

– his penmanship is passable and his taste isn't terrible. If you're born in this era and live in Beijing, you're probably going to become a bit self-obsessed, nothing unusual about that. At his age I was still confusedly trying to live like a normal person. That's why I kept taking my dog to all kinds of vets – I was trying to show that I was a kind, compassionate person, lying to myself, pretending that no matter what happened I would never abandon him, promising him we'd definitely go for a walk the next day, but once again I'd fail to get out of bed early enough. I log into my email account after a long search for the password, which turns out to be my mother's landline number. There are two unread emails, one from a college student who says she will be passing through S———, and would I like to buy her dinner? It's from three years ago. I didn't see it at the time and presumably she didn't starve to death, so neither of us missed anything. The other message is five minutes old. No preamble, just the opening of a novel:

Dear traveller, I sing you this song. The lyrics have long been lost, but the melody comes from ancient times, and I will fill it with random words in the hope of amusing you.

I'm a carpenter, oh, I have three axes
Not just three axes, I have a child too
The child's mother died long ago
Each year I put flowers on her grave
The child is now a young woman
Her hair curls and she stands tall as my shoulder
All may love her, no need for my permission
As long as their songs are as stirring as mine
And they wield their axes more expertly than I
Pour me a cup of the finest wine
And I will tell you my daughter's every thought

At this, the killer put away his knife. Let me see your daughter then, he said. My daughter has a cold and has fallen behind, said the man. I doubt she'll reach the way station before midnight. How do I know it'll be her and not some accomplice? said the killer. I've been on the run for over a decade, said the man, I have no friends left. You need to spend time with friends to keep them, which you can't do if you're always on the road. Why shouldn't I just kill you now? said the killer. I can simply take your daughter when she gets here. When she gets here, I'll write a letter entrusting her to you, said the man. Then everything will be above board, and you'll have nothing to worry about for the rest of your life. So when do I kill you? said the killer. In front of your daughter? Won't she hate me for it? I'll kill myself, said the man. I've got the poison ready, it's in this cup of wine right here. Bury me by the side of the road, no gravestone, come back to the way station and wash your hands, then take her with you. The killer rested his clasped hands on his knee. What does your daughter look like? he said. Fat or thin? Large eyes or small? Blue eyes, said the man. Why does she have blue eyes? said the killer. What colour were her mother's eyes? Black, like mine, said the man. Didn't you meet her? No, said the killer. Her eyes were black as coal and bright as the stars, said the man. Whenever she was lost in thought they would move in their sockets like tumbling dice. So how come your daughter has blue eyes? said the killer. I don't know, said the man. She was born with blue eyes, and curly hair, and skin as white as milk. As she grew older her eyes became bluer, her skin paler and her hair curlier. An icy wind rattled the battered way station door. The innkeeper had fled a long time ago. Two stallions were tied to the doorpost, one fat and one thin. The man added a few logs to the fire, while the killer braced the door with a stone. Through a crack, he could see the snow outside and hear his horse stamping its hooves.

That's all. Neatly typed, almost like calligraphy, no typos and no title. I stand and walk around my study, then open the door to get a glass of water. Wu Song takes the opportunity to dart in. He leaps onto the desk and stares at the computer screen. He does this whenever I'm not quick enough to stop him, sometimes reaching out a paw to type random symbols. After some thought, I reply:

Hi, I read what you sent me. It's interesting. Several parts of the plot don't quite make sense, though if you think about them long enough they sort of work. Your narrative voice is taut – this doesn't read like it's by someone who's never written fiction before. I was a little rude to you today, or maybe I should say dismissive. I didn't think you'd be so accomplished. If you really did just write this, I take my hat off to you. One thing – have you plotted out the rest of the story yet? Writing a novel is like flying a kite: you might be able to get it off the ground, but how high it soars is all down to technique. It doesn't matter why the killer wants to take the man's life, but the daughter will be the key to the whole thing. I'm curious to know whether she shows up, and if she does, what happens? You mentioned that I'd influenced you, and I don't want to get ahead of myself, but could this have been inspired by my early story about the assassin pursuing the carpenter? My plotting then was too rigidly logical – the carpenter was destined to die because he'd constructed a vicious torture device – not as free-spirited as this. To be frank, I love this opening and very much look forward to reading more. With best wishes.

Wu Song lies quietly by my side, no longer causing mischief. The reply comes right away, and consists of only two words:

Still writing.

I make myself more tea, but when it's ready I realize I don't actually want it. I clean this room every day, but somehow it's always an unholy mess. That's a structural problem with life – even as you tidy one thing up you never know what chaos you might be causing elsewhere.

I once dated an outstanding Italian translator. She understood Italian superbly and could transform it into even better Mandarin. She translated several dense books of criticism, all of which I loved. I met her at an event and found her quite ordinary-looking: no make-up, short curly hair, book clutched to her chest, unremarkable long dress covered in creases. Her toes poked out of her sandals; half the red polish had chipped off her nails. I went over to express my admiration. She nodded and said, I know you, you write very long sentences.

– Maybe that's because I've read too many foreign novels.

– And yet you look like a short sentence.

– What does that mean?

– It's your chin. Your chin looks like a short sentence with only one verb.

– Which verb?

– Cut. As in cut down.

– Sounds like I ought to try cutting my sentences down.

– Have you heard of Giovanni Verga? He's an Italian writer.

– No.

– He wrote that 'when things grow too long they turn into snakes'.

– Interesting. But your translations are full of snakes.

– If the source text is snakes I have to tangle with snakes. Whereas you ought to be constructing your own style. Maybe that's silly of me to say – you're older than me. I bet that makes you want to stop talking to me.

– No, the opposite.

I thought about it for a second: what would the opposite be? Finally I said, It makes me want to talk to you even more.

I was due on stage in fifteen minutes, but I didn't make it. My editor accepted the award on my behalf, an honour for my long sentences. The translator took care of me, bought me shirts in the right size, corrected the mistakes in my thinking, pointed out the weak links in my writing. I learned how to make salads, use verbs correctly and blow-dry her hair. When we broke up, I said, I can't go any further with you because I'm only able to lead one kind of life, to be one kind of person. Why can't you be happier? she asked. Why can't you become a better person? That's my tragedy, I said. Weakness is the opium of my spirit. When I'm with you I don't feel like doing anything, like I'm an alcoholic. Will you miss me on your deathbed? she said. It's possible, I said. Or maybe I'll think of a sentence I haven't finished writing. Tomorrow morning at eight, she said, I'll go to the street corner outside my house, and I'll wait for you there till eight at night. If you don't come, I'll forget you. It might rain tomorrow, I said. Let's just end things now. Eight o'clock tomorrow, she said. Then she placed her key on my desk and left. The next day the sun shone brightly from dawn till dusk, without a drop of rain. A wind rose in the evening. It was autumn then, the ginkgo tree outside my window had lost its leaves and its branches were shivering. I sat at home the whole day long, fully dressed, and never made it out the door. A little past seven, someone knocked. I ran to open the door. It was the six-year-old boy from next door holding up a wedge of cake: it was his birthday. His father had walked out on them, leaving them with this huge apartment. The boy wore flip-flops and a paper crown. Do you remember, he said, one time in the elevator I tripped over my bicycle and you stopped me from falling. That was nothing, I said. All I had to do was reach out my arm. Well now we're even, he said. His mother was leaning against the doorway, watching as her son placed the slice of cake in my hand.

I ate the cake, drank some wine, took notes on a book I was reading and dozed off.

An hour later, a second email arrives:

The man took off his boots and rested his feet by the fireside, roasting his soles. The flames scorched his socks, they tightened and wrinkled like sweet potatoes. Ever since I sensed you were chasing me, said the man, I haven't taken off my boots. The snow is getting heavier, said the killer. How will your daughter get here? Relax, said the man. We arranged to meet here, she'll definitely arrive tonight. Have a drink. Warm yourself up. I didn't put anything in your drink – if you want I'll taste some to prove it. Fine, said the killer. Go ahead. The man picked up the second cup, took a gulp and handed it to the killer, who started sipping from it. My dear future son-in-law, said the man, you're far too anxious. Your eyes haven't rested in any spot for longer than three seconds. Have you ever killed someone? asked the killer. Never, said the man. Though I've watched a lot of people die. I've killed seventeen people, said the killer. Twelve men, three women and two children. Different every time. I remember the exact moment of their deaths, what they wore, how they looked, their last words. My memory is sharp, that's why I'm not suited to this line of work. But I'm a great swordsman, I have no family, and I wanted to buy a plot of land to build a house, so here we are. What did they say before they died? asked the man. When I barged in, a five-year-old boy hid the candy-man he was eating under his pillow, said the killer. He wanted me to finish it after I'd killed him. Did you? asked

*the man. Yes, said the killer. It was a Monkey King.
Its head had melted and was stuck to the pillow.
Was it sweet? Yes, the sweetest thing I ever tasted,
said the killer. It improved my mood no end. Back
outside I found a well and drank a lot of water. Is
your daughter coming on horseback? Yes, said the
man, I spent my life savings on that horse. Oh, I
forgot to tell you, but she has a disease. What disease? asked the killer anxiously. She sheds her skin,
said the man. What do you mean? said the killer.
Ever since she turned twenty, she's shed her skin
every twelve months, said the man. After moulting,
she looks the same as she did the year before. She'll
never get old? said the killer. That's right, said the
man. Does that please you? Yes, said the killer. This
drink is delicious, you should try some. Well, how
about that? After all these years of being a killer,
things are finally going my way. That's the virtue of
persistence, said the man. If you do something long
enough, you'll eventually run into some good luck.*

I reply immediately:

*Friend, you're great at detail, and you have the
courage to slow your story down. Both of these are
good qualities. I've been writing for a long time,*

and I've only recently understood that fiction isn't a simplified sketch of reality's highs and lows, but rather a spiritual egg that needs slow incubation. The human spirit is chaotic, aimless, nuanced, and it hovers in unobtrusive places. What did Emily Dickinson say? 'A Letter always feels to me like immortality because it is the mind alone without corporeal friend.' You've written a story that I wish I'd written, or rather I should say, you've written a story that resonates with me, which brings me joy. When I first started writing I faced obstacles on all sides, I didn't belong anywhere, I had no one to rely on. All I could do was force myself to keep going, to submit draft after draft. Finally an editor replied. I stayed up all night making the revisions she'd suggested. The next morning, I put all my effort into writing her the most beautiful email. I probably worked on that message even more than on my story. Before I could hit send, she wrote again to say her boss had seen my submission and didn't feel it had potential, so I should forget about it. But I could write something else, she said, and send it directly to her. After I was done crying, I started another piece. I'm telling you this not in order to show how resilient I am – in fact, I frequently feel like giving up, but I can't find any other work that suits me. There's no other way of spending my life that I could feel any passion for. So this is a passive choice. I feel like everyone else picked their careers and I'm stuck with what's left. I remember your face. It's narrow, unscrupulous, gleaming with arrogance. I loathe your face, but I have to admit it's the sort of face an author ought to have. You're luckier than I was. Through your brashness and self-aggrandizement you managed to meet me, and I just so happen to have nothing better to do this evening than to read your work. It's very satisfactory so far, and if you stick the landing, I'll recommend you to all the editors I know. I'll help you in any way I can, though if your luck is as bad as mine, my help might just be a mousetrap. Think hard about your life: how much are you willing to sacrifice? How much selfishness and isolation can you endure? Of course I'm not saying you need to answer these questions right now. I hope the rest of your story doesn't disappoint. It's not that I'm particularly concerned about your future, I just don't want to have wasted my evening. With best wishes.

I wait a while, but there's no response. I fill the blank space with other tasks, answering WeChat messages and making appointments. I check the inbox again:

still no reply. I mop the floor and vacuum cat fur. All of a sudden I remember that it must be time to put on the heating at my mother's house. By this time of year it's already freezing up north, and the streets are empty of pedestrians at night. I call to ask her if she has fuel money. If she doesn't, I'll wire her some. But she doesn't answer. Probably watching serials with her phone on silent, perched on the foot of her bed two paces from the TV. Sometimes I dream about her. She used to be very strong. She could cycle an hour in the icy wind, front basket full of groceries, me perched on the rear. By the time we got home, her face would be ruddy and she'd be in high spirits, pulling off her coat and starting to cook right away. Nowadays her eyes droop and she sits around all day, swaddled in warm clothes.

Friends from my teenage years populate my dreams – all of us sobbing after the tide turns and we lose a soccer match. People I met after thirty rarely show up in my dreams. I've lost touch with my old friends in real life, but to my subconscious they're treasured antiques, constantly polished and carefully re-examined. One time I dreamed about the Italian translator. She was working on a very thin pamphlet, but somehow she couldn't finish it. Her hair turned white, and still she kept working. I was at her side, shouting, Stop, please stop. She ignored me, the fountain pen in her hand moving as if it was battery-operated. When I prodded her, she slammed the book into my face and said, Take a good look at this, it's yours. Your dogshit ideas, your desire to be understood, your urge to escape, all dogshit. I'm exhausted, my neck aches, and you don't care one bit. When I woke up, I reached across the pillow beside me and found myself alone in the bed.

Wu Song has fallen asleep with his tail flopped across my keyboard and I carefully move it. Unlike other cats, he doesn't startle when you touch his tail. His little triangular mouth is slightly open, neck curled into his body like he's in a coma. I check my email again and find a new message:

Cold seeped in beneath the door, but the fire was ferocious. Let's change places, said the killer. That way I can keep an eye on the door. The man was a little drunk, his eyes narrowing, and he had a smile on his face. All right, he said, I can see you've thought of everything. After that they were silent, and the killer didn't drink another drop as he waited for midnight. The man kept emptying his glass. Now and then he'd smile and shake his head. Abruptly he said, I was lying earlier. Once again the killer tensed. *What about? I* have *killed someone, said the man. Who? The first killer they sent after me, said the man. She pursued me for two years, and finally caught up with me one night at a way station much like this one. She was armed with a pair of mallets. What happened? asked the killer. I calmed her down, said the man. I was younger then, not yet eroded by the harsh winds of time. I pleaded with her. She knew I couldn't beat her in a fight, so she let her guard down and we talked. And then? said the killer. Did you poison her? No, said the man, I made her fall in love with me. She'd been chasing me for so long she knew me inside out, and that was a good enough foundation to build our love on. All it took was a nudge. That's a killer's greatest taboo, said the killer. You might as well say the greatest mistake, said the man. Chasing a target for so long that you're no longer capable of finishing him off. What happened next? said the killer. I asked her to come with me, and we fled together. We were on the run for two years. I kept trying to find ways to kill her, but she was too strong. She slept lightly and she never fell ill. Why kill her? asked the killer. She'd already paid a big price to be with you. But she'd still intended to kill me, said the man. Eventually she got pregnant. After she gave birth, I took the baby from her, then I killed her. The killer ran his fingers along his blade, speechless. She was still smiling when I killed her, said the man. What a silly woman. My daughter will be here soon. Do you need to wash your hair? No, said the killer. The man's head swayed as he hummed a tune:*

I'm a carpenter, oh, I have three axes
Not just three axes, I have a child too
The child's mother died long ago
Each year I put flowers on her grave
The child is now a young woman
Her hair curls and she stands tall as my shoulder

More time passed. The flames died down. The man dozed off, clutching at his shirt and mumbling softly. From outside came the muffled thud of hooves on snow, then the snort of a horse coming to a halt. A moment later, someone pushed at the door and knocked three times. Firelight illuminated the grimy wrinkles of the killer's face, his greasy collar, the clothes he had no one to wash for him. His bright blade was the only clean part of him.

I don't reply right away, but light a cigarette. I'm worried the ending will be too good. I know it won't be weak, but it shouldn't be too good either. It's the small hours of the morning, but I'm not at all tired. An old man is walking his dog downstairs, kicking his legs out high as he goes. I wait an hour, but my inbox remains empty.

Please send me the ending as soon as possible. At this point in the story, it needn't be too long. The editors will be at their desks soon.

No response.

There are several possibilities: (i) The man and his daughter team up to kill the killer and flee together. (ii) The killer kills the man and takes the daughter away. (iii) The killer kills the man but the daughter refuses to cooperate so she gets killed too, and the killer leaves dejected. (iv) The person at the door isn't the daughter. All these scenarios make sense and would work fine. Please hurry up and finish.

No response.

It's been two days. You must have finished the story by now. I have no idea what you're playing at. How much time have I spent giving you feedback and encouraging you? I've spoken to some editors and we're all eagerly awaiting the ending. I'm not asking for acknowledgement, I just want you to respect your own labour. Whether a story is good or bad, the most important thing is that it has an ending. I haven't slept in two days. That's not your fault, I've always been a light sleeper. I want to know how the story ends, even if the ending's dogshit. I won't be able to sleep till I know what happens. Maybe you were too tired to write before, but you must have rested by now, so please finish the story and send it to me. I'm waiting.

I managed to eat something, but I haven't cleaned the apartment for four days now. I sleep a little, but wake up after fifteen minutes, convinced that a strange woman is by my side, full of sexual desire. I've been writing for almost ten years, waiting for an ending, just as everyone else on earth is busy with their own lives, waiting for it all to be over. If you've had a heart attack and died, give me a sign: make my desk lamp flicker, make it snow. If you're alive, please write to me. Even if you won't send me the ending, at least say something, anything at all. I miss you, my friend. I feel like I'm missing someone who's forgotten about me long ago. Are you still alive? Are you still a normal person, filled with countless desires? That's okay. No need to get too serious. If someone's trying to kill you, please tell me. I keep a horse tucked away in my safe and I can ride to your rescue anytime.

I jerk awake once again. A strong wind is blowing outside, and the bare branches tremble. The sky is dark, and in the distance car lights glitter like phosphorescence. I glance at my watch. I've slept for a whole half hour. Wu Song snoozes beside me, still looking unconscious. Has he lost weight? Noticing I'm awake, he blinks his eyes open and a purr rumbles in his throat. I feel hunger and an immense weariness, as if I've been dragging a millstone behind me for years, and am covered in rope burns. I sit bolt upright and look at my watch again: fifteen minutes to eight. I tumble out of bed, throw on a coat and rush out the door. I'm still limping, and I haven't had time to tie my laces, but I fly along. A shower of happiness drenches me. Someone's waiting for me. She's been waiting a long time and must be close to despair, the flames are guttering, but I know she won't leave till time is up, she won't give up, and me, I'm almost there.

Mars

WEI MINGLEI GETS INTO THE PASSENGER SEAT
and fastens his seatbelt. He doesn't utter a word
the whole ride until they are almost at Gao Hong's
hotel, when he abruptly turns to the driver and says,
Stop, I want to go back. The driver spent the first ten
minutes chatting away animatedly: Shan Tianfang
died, you know, the pingshu storyteller, now it feels
weird listening to his pingshu, do you ever feel like
that? We have to stop this trade war with America,
look at that big supermarket at New World, closed
down just like that, a perfectly good supermarket,
all because of that little monkey Jack Ma, does that
make any sense to you? Minglei didn't respond.
He wasn't on his phone or asleep or looking at the
scenery, he was just sitting perfectly still, staring
directly ahead through the windscreen, which was
still streaky from when it rained earlier, like the
sticky strip of an envelope. The sky was pitch black

and there wasn't much traffic. The driver eventually gave up, wondering if there was something wrong with his passenger's ears. You want to go back? he says now. Yes, says Minglei, back the same way. You'll have to call another taxi, says the driver. I'll pay you, don't worry, says Minglei. I know, says the driver, you don't look like the cheating type, but I live nearby, just down that road over there. So please find another taxi, I'm done for the day. Minglei glances at his watch: 1.45 a.m. He pays the fare, shoulders his black rucksack and gets out, watching the taxi turn down an alleyway and drive around some trash. He keeps watching till the tail lights are gone.

The hotel Gao Hong is staying at is over ninety storeys. Quite a few young people in sharp suits are standing around the lobby, all of them wearing earpieces which don't seem to affect their chattering. A few are standing in a row, looking like the same person at different ages, chasing away any vehicles that linger too long by the entrance. Despite the late hour, there is a constant stream of people and cars, stopping and starting. Someone sticks his head out of his car window to continue an argument, but quickly winds it up and drives off when the other person walks over. A strapping foreigner gets out of his car, followed by a tiny, toy-like child. Someone clutching a laptop speaks non-stop into her Bluetooth headset as she strides into the lobby, apparently piloting by instinct. Minglei teaches PE at an elementary school. He used to be a soccer player until a tiny fracture in his heel left him unable to sprint or jump. Now he teaches children to play soccer. Mostly he leads the fun, blowing the whistle when necessary, resolving disputes. He always makes sure the kids warm up. If not for his injury, he could have been a top-notch goalie. He's not very tall, but no one could stop a ground shot like he could. Despite not being particularly outgoing, he was somehow able to quickly win the trust of the defenders, who took his advice on strategy and only passed the ball to him when they had no other choice. Their coach nicknamed him The Safe. He really did seem to have a future in the sport.

He glances at his phone. Still no reply from Gao Hong. She told him this morning that her event was only a five-minute drive away, but she'd be coming from the underground car park so he should wait for her by the entrance and she'd text when she was almost there. The tall, narrow building is at the junction of two streets, across from a brightly lit shopping mall which is now closed, though the luxury-goods store on the ground floor still glitters extravagantly, as if all those riches have given it insomnia. Minglei hasn't travelled much since turning twenty, but he went to many cities as a soccer player, including a ho-hum match in Shanghai in which his fist connected with an opposing player's browbone during an aerial duel. That's his only memory of this game, a guy around his age resentfully pulling away, bleeding.

Gao Hong was his classmate in junior high. Their school was well-known for its slack discipline, an openness that came from being closed off. They were a branch campus of a local high school where everyone from Year Two onwards boarded and were only allowed home once a week. With this many young men and women locked up in the foothills outside the city, it made no difference how many rules or teachers you had. Between the shelves of the library, in the far corners of the sports fields, beneath the mosquito nets of their dorms, many of the students came to an intimate understanding of their own and other people's bodies. Vast quantities of messages flew between classmates, between different faculties, between students in different years. Sometimes words could be more stimulating than bodies. These letters – no envelopes or stamps necessary – were passed from hand to hand, left in drawers, dropped or thrown to their recipients, fostering many short-lived relationships. As soon as they left the foothills, all these emotions suddenly lost their power, like when a dam is demolished and a river's turbulence calms. Still, Minglei nurtures the memories in his heart like beloved pets, never letting them loose for even a moment. Vast murals fade and chip away, but Minglei's recollections proliferate endlessly. He could have made more memories, but in his final year his prowess at soccer led to him being transferred to a sports school, fate spiriting him away like a human trafficker. A few years after that, the branch campus was closed down by the authorities and turned into a hot-springs resort. The dorms and library were demolished and replaced by little chalets, and the playing fields were turned into a pool. Only the boiler room remained intact.

Minglei weighs up whether he ought to keep standing here, ten metres from the entrance, or if he should go into the lobby and sit down. He hesitates for so long that he realizes twenty minutes have passed, and he decides to stay put. September in Shanghai is fairly warm, and there are quite a few drunken people about. The occasional pedestrian ventures carefully onto the road, keeping a close eye on approaching vehicles. Minglei turns his phone over in his hands like meditation beads. He was married once, followed by a placid separation. No kids. The problem arose during an overseas business trip that his ex-wife went on. There's no point discussing this sort of thing. They fell in love in the first place because they had a shared understanding of the world, which continued even then. Minglei kept their apartment, which had been his to start with, and his ex-wife took the car. They'd known each other for twelve years, dated for five and been married for two. It only took three days to go from reaching a consensus to finalizing the divorce proceedings. Afterwards, he noticed he could no longer see his ex-wife's social media feed, while his remained wide open to her. He waited a few days, then finally he blocked her too.

Several times now he's woken in the night feeling like he might die, not from sadness, but in a fire or earthquake or from a heart attack, or the overhead lamp crashing down on top of him – but so what? It would just be him dying alone in a double bed, no one to rescue him or even call for help. He wonders if he's missed anything over the last dozen years. His ex had matured, he realizes, complexity and mysteriousness creeping into her personality and her way of interacting with the world, while he remained the same old person. His greatest pleasure is still snagging a pair of newly dropped sneakers, even though he can't run very fast any more. Whenever one of his students masters some footwork, he'll dream about it that night, which makes him want to phone his ex to tell her how much effort he's putting into his work, and that the team he supports has made it into the Euro finals and now he's anxious their coach will start them in a formation different to the one Minglei's envisioned, leaving them vulnerable to the other side's traps. Living alone in the apartment he claimed back, there are times when he gets confused and thinks he's still a teenager or has become an old man – some other person than the one he is now. His present feels like the past but also the future. Maybe he's gotten a bit strange from being so normal. What if he thinks he's orbiting the sun but actually he's just rotating on his own axis? Maybe he's nowhere near the rest of humanity, far from the direction everyone else is heading in. But how did that happen? He feels a flash of despair, followed by a glow of pride. So be it, he thinks. I don't owe anyone anything. I'm no accountant, but if someone is keeping a ledger somewhere I definitely won't be in the debtors' column. I've cleared

my mind and I accept that I myself – myself, my self
– am all that I possess.

Around 2.15, Gao Hong texts to say she's on her
way back, where is he? He says he's almost at the
hotel but traffic is bad. At this hour? she says. Road-
works, he says. They've dug up the whole surface.
I'll be past it soon. I'll go straight to my room from
the parking lot, she says. Wait in the lobby. A young
man in a hoodie will come and get you. What are
you wearing? A blue Adidas tracksuit, he says. I'm
175 centimetres. She replies with a thumbs up. He
tucks his phone back into his pocket and heads into
the foyer, rucksack pressing on his back as if it's pro-
pelling him forward. There is a pool in the centre of
the room in which brightly coloured koi swim. No
sooner has he stopped walking than a young man
in a hoodie approaches. Mr Wei? He leads Minglei
to the elevator, which speeds up to the eighty-fifth
floor. Minglei's ears are popping, but the young man
seems used to it, and keeps his phone pressed to his
face the whole time. Now he brings it to his lips and
says, I told you, it's not possible. You've said too
much, everyone's going to know it's coming from
you, so what's the point? Don't you understand?
They reach the room and the young man rings the
bell, then turns to Minglei and asks, Where have you

come from? Before Minglei can answer, the door opens and a young woman with large eyes says to Hoodie, Got the melatonin? No one told me to buy melatonin, he says. Stop talking nonsense and go get some, she says. Stupid bitch, he says as he departs. Mr Wei? says the girl. Yes, Minglei says. I'm sorry, but I need to see some ID, she says. He fishes his ID from his wallet and hands it over. She glances at it, slips it into her trouser pocket and says, This way, please. Miss Jingya has been waiting. She twisted her ankle stepping offstage tonight, so she couldn't come get you herself. The suite is very warm, and the girl is in a T-shirt that reveals her gleaming, smooth arms. The slogan on the T-shirt reads *Art is limitless debauchery* over a drawing of a man having his belt removed.

Gao Hong must have written Minglei three hundred letters about every aspect of her life during their time at school, yet they were never terribly close. Many people back then intermingled freely, but the two of them always remained as separate as a carton of apple juice and a carton of orange juice. They didn't use nicknames or endearments, it was always, Hello Gao Hong, Hello Wei Minglei, followed by whatever they wanted to say and a question for the other person. If Minglei remembers right, it all started because of a mistake: he got a letter intended for Dai Minglei, another boy in his class, and, not noticing the error, replied to it. Soon the two of them forgot Dai Minglei and became frequent correspondents. Gao Hong's recollection, on the other hand, is that she didn't know Dai Minglei at all and had no interest in writing to him. She'd seen Wei Minglei in a soccer match and found him as dashing as a great admiral. Rock solid, unlike the other boys, who were far too anxious to show off. That's why she decided to write to him, but a slip of the pen led her to address the message to Dai Minglei instead. One truth, two explanations. That was the first subject of their letters: whether their connection was the result of a major misunderstanding or just an error of detail. This was highly amusing to both of them.

When Gao Hong began acting she took the stage name Gao Jingya, and moved from theatre to film and TV. Her career path was defined by self-awareness and coincidence, with too many twists and turns to list. By this point she's become responsible for the livelihoods of a whole group of people, like a parent. She's thirty-six, the best age, but also the most dangerous age. No one – including her manager, her assistant, her make-up artist and her family – has any idea why she suddenly remembered the letters she wrote to Minglei back in junior high. She never wrote to anyone else before or since, just those hundreds of letters to him. Why didn't she recall them another time? Why did it happen out of the blue on this perfectly ordinary morning, so urgently that she grabbed her assistant and said they had to track down this guy to find out if the letters still existed? When Minglei said yes, they still existed, he hadn't lost a single one, her assistant felt like the sky was falling, but he also had to admire Miss Jingya's meticulous thinking – most people are scared of the future, but she'd realized the true danger lay in the past. Classy as always, Gao Hong personally sought out Minglei on WeChat, bought him a first-class ticket to Shanghai, and asked him to personally deliver the letters to her. You might as well bring them all, she texted enigmatically. It won't feel right if a single one is missing. I need the complete set.

The girl with the skinny arms asks what he'd like to drink. He says water, and she brings him a glass of warm water just as Gao Hong emerges from the bedroom. She is taller than she was in high school and has more hair now. She is thickly made up, dressed in a long-sleeved white shirt and cropped black trousers that reveal impeccably white calves, and mauve slippers that tie the whole outfit together. One ankle is wrapped in a thick bandage that goes so well with her clothes it might as well be an accessory. Gao Hong extends a hand and says, Hello Wei Minglei. He gently takes her hand between his palms and says, Hello Gao Hong. You haven't changed, she says. How are things going? Did you have a good trip? Yes, thanks, he says. Could I have my ID back? What ID? she says. That girl accidentally put my ID into her own pocket, he says. Lingzi! calls Gao Hong, but no one answers – the girl has slipped away without them noticing. Where'd she go? says Minglei. She'll be back soon, says Gao Hong. They have to deal with a lot of stuff, mistakes happen, sorry about that. Actually you have changed a little. You're more articulate now. Wasn't I before? says Minglei. You used to speak all broken up – it wasn't a stutter, just not smooth, says Gao Hong. Or maybe I'm remembering wrong, we never did talk much. Did you bring the letters? Yes, all 312 of them, says Minglei. That should be all.

He observes himself as he speaks. Am I articulate? I was tense just now, like I wanted to pee, but I'm slowly calming down. Why? Gao Jingya is no

longer the person he knew back in high school, and
perhaps that's why he can relax a little. When she
appeared, Minglei looked closely at her and for a
moment felt he'd entered the wrong room. Could
this really be Gao Hong? At first he thought she'd
just grown taller and acquired a more sophisti-
cated hairstyle, but now he notices that her eyes are
a different shape, her lips are thicker and her chin
has shrunk. All of this is understandable – in her
line of work, you have to invest in your face. The
strange thing is her neck seems longer too, and her
shoulders are narrower. How are her legs so long
and straight? He remembers her in school, her long
torso and those stubby legs that made her seem tall
when she was sitting but short when she stood. Does
surgery to elongate your neck even exist? He begins
to wonder whether celebrities use body doubles for
moments like this, as well as for dangerous stunts.
That would be bad. Do I seem dangerous to her?
The question didn't occur to him on the drive here,
but everything that's happened since he stepped
through the door has made him understand he is
a perilous figure indeed. That's right, he represents
the power of the past, which makes him the assassin
of the present, a witness she has no defence against.
Shall I order you something to eat? she asks. He

doesn't reply, but continues staring at her. I don't know this neighbourhood, she says. We can see if anywhere around here has good ratings. With that she picks up her phone. He looks at her drooping lashes and feels the pointlessness of his defilement, his worry. This is Gao Hong. She didn't stretch her neck after becoming an actor, her neck got longer and then she started acting.

– I'm not hungry. Here are the letters, have a look. If there's nothing wrong, I'll go.

– Do you have somewhere else to be?

– No.

– You came here just for me, didn't you? You weren't passing through like you said on WeChat.

– Yes.

– Then there's no rush. Let's look at them together.

She takes the letters he produces from his rucksack and spreads them on the coffee table.

– Look, the envelopes are from the university my ba taught at. He had a stroke, he can't speak any more.

– When did that happen?

– Don't pretend like you care. He came to the school to have a look at you, you know.

– He came to see me?

– He read some of your letters and wanted to know what kind of person you were.

–What did he say after he read them?

– Nothing at all. But this year, just two days before the stroke, he suddenly brought you up. I have no idea why. He was doing the dishes and out of nowhere he said, What's that Wei boy up to now? The one who ended all his letters with *respectfully yours*? To be quite honest, when he said your name I hadn't thought about you in years. You don't mind, do you?

– Not at all, it just makes me a bit sad.

– No need for that. You've never met him so your sadness is pure humanism, it means nothing. I usually have a drink before bed, want something? Or are you going to pretend to refuse so I have to ask you again?

–No, I'll have a drink. And that wasn't humanism, I'm sad because he's your father. That's different.

Gao Hong ignores this last sentence and stands to get some champagne from the fridge.

–This one's a bit sweet, is that okay?

–That's fine. I've never had champagne before.

– There aren't any glasses. Let's drink out of teacups.

Minglei can hold his liquor well but he doesn't

enjoy drinking, perhaps because his early ath-
letic training has left him with a high metabolism,
which means the alcohol is never in his system long
enough to grant him the release and exhilaration
that would allow him to act like a different person. Quite the opposite, he becomes more lucid the
more he drinks, and begins chewing on problems
he was previously able to ignore. When he drinks he
speaks less and less, sinking into melancholy and
heavy-heartedness. He got through huge quantities
of beer and red wine on his wedding day, and played
so many drinking games that the young men from
the bride's family were left completely smashed. In
the bridal chamber he felt hollowed out. His wife
was exhausted and quickly drifted off, while he lay
awake for some reason, feeling like a hypocritical
person in a hypocritical world, not knowing why
he felt this way. By the time he woke the next day,
the alcohol had worn off and he was able to forget
the whole thing.

Gao Hong raises her champagne and clinks her
teacup against his.

– Thanks for coming.

– No problem.

She swigs half her cup down and he does the
same. To be honest, I'm a bit of an alcoholic, says

Gao Hong. I can't get to sleep without a drink. Actually I can't get to sleep with one either, so I might as well drink, right?

– You have a high-pressure job. Me, I fall asleep as soon as my head touches the pillow, though sleeping is a bit pointless anyway.

– Do you still play soccer?

– Very seldom. I have a steel rod in my leg. These days I teach little kids to play ball.

– Do you like kids?

– Yes. If you knew them, you'd like them too.

– Not necessarily. I only have a little bit of love and I keep it for myself. In one of your letters, you said we shouldn't only love ourselves and trust each other, but that we ought to go out and love other people too.

She gulps down the rest of her champagne and refills her cup.

– Did I really say that?

– Yes. It's somewhere in that pile of letters. Let's read them now. Pick one at random.

– Forget it. I should go, I have a plane to catch tomorrow.

Gao Hong plucks an envelope from the stack and notices that it's sealed with red wax.

– Did we really do this?

– No, I did that afterwards.

– What for?

– I had no choice. If it wasn't sealed something might escape.

– When did you become like this?

– Let me see which one that is. Right, it's the one with a bird.

– If it flies out, will it be able to get back in?

– Depends.

Gao Hong scrapes off the wax and a black mynah darts from the envelope, no larger than her palm. It alights by the living-room mirror. She cries out and jumps to her feet, dropping the envelope. Minglei bends to pick it up. Don't lose this, he says. The mynah is strutting around, peering at itself in the mirror. Suddenly it says, What lies beneath the gold? Its reflection replies, Who are you asking, fatso? The mynah says again, What lies beneath the gold? The reflection replies, Your momma, fatso. This seems to amuse the mynah, who chuckles smugly. How are you doing this? says Gao Hong, terrified. I'm not doing anything, he says. I told you, this was in the envelope all along. Who are you? she says. Wei Minglei, he says. I'm calling for help, she says, I don't know who you are. How did you get in here? Lingzi? Lingzi! No response. Minglei holds out his ID and says, Look, I'm the person you've been looking for. Didn't you say Lingzi took your ID? she says. I just got it back, he says. Don't be scared, if you answer the mynah's questions it will return to the envelope. That's right, fatso, says the mynah. What lies beneath the gold? I don't know, says Gao Hong. It's a Turkish proverb, says Minglei. You've been to Turkey, haven't you? I remember you did a show there. It's just a mynah. Are you afraid of birds? Gao Hong is standing pressed against the wall, her injured leg curled up against her. Beneath the gold lies silver, she says. That's rich, says the mynah. You want it all, do you? Gold *and* silver? Gao Hong stares at the mynah and says, Wait, that's the mynah I once had. It got diarrhoea and died. Minglei says, Your line is: My bird died, and I suspect my ma poisoned it because I loved it too much. While no one was looking, I buried it in a planter outside the school building so I could walk past it every day. I've got it, says Gao Hong. Beneath the gold lies a scorpion. The mynah twirls around and crows, Beddy-bye! The reflection is still for a moment, then it takes a leap and dives straight into the envelope.

Minglei stands and says, I'm sorry I gave you a fright. That's just how these envelopes are. It's no trick. They've tortured me for years, and now they're yours. Gao Hong sits and covers her face with her hands. No way, she says, please take them away. I've been looking after them for twenty years, says Minglei. I've gone to a lot of trouble to bring them here, I can't take them back now. I'm begging you, she says. Like you just said, he says, do we even know each other? I'll burn them, she says. Minglei is silent. The envelopes begin to tremble, then they rise up into rows and march around the coffee table like parading troops. Some are a little torn and lag behind. Less than a minute later, they slump back into a pile. Would you like to have a rest in the bedroom? says Gao Hong. You can leave in the morning. I have my own room, says Minglei. Do you remember the last letter you wrote? Or maybe I should ask: why didn't we keep writing to each other? I've forgotten, says Gao Hong, but that was always going to end, wasn't it? She's been drinking steadily, and her eyes are beginning to droop. A greasy sheen blooms across her skin. As she drinks, her little pink tongue darts from the corners of her lips, and out of nowhere a smile surges across her face. She can barely suppress her desire. Her legs are clamped together as if she's trying to lock something away. She leans away from her chair, dabbing at the sweat on her long, slender neck. I've never slept with a magician, she says. Can magic appear from anywhere at all? Let's look at the final letter, if you're not too tired, says Minglei. Obviously I'm not tired, says Gao Hong. Sleep is such a waste. I'm full of energy. I can stay awake for as long as I like. She is no longer quivering with fear, now that she has accepted the situation. Minglei senses that she is developing an attachment to him, the source of her terror. Perhaps this is a habit of hers? He is ashamed, but also feels he got what he came for.

Minglei pulls a letter from the bottom of the pile. One corner is a little torn, but it's been patched with white paper. He grabs the box of matches from the ashtray and lights one, using the flame to soften the wax seal, then gently prises open the envelope. A rope slides out and crawls across the table. An ordinary length of hemp rope, over a metre long, the only unusual thing about it is that it's brand new. Give it some time and it'd look like any other length of rope. Gao Hong points at it and laughs. Rope, she says. Why is it so warm? says the rope. We're in the south, says Gao Hong. I need to wash my face, says the rope. It dips itself into Gao Hong's champagne, wetting one end, then slinks over to the fridge and pulls the door open to enjoy the cool air. It's cute, says Gao Hong. What did you say? says the rope. I said you're quite sexy, she says. The rope abruptly tautens into a straight line. And now? it says. Pervert, says Gao Hong. You've forgotten quite a few things, says Minglei. Shut up, she says, shut your fucking mouth. Oh good, says the rope, everyone's saying what they really think. Hmm? I haven't finished, says Gao Hong. Even when I'm pissing, I fantasize about drowning you. Do you believe me? Minglei nods, perhaps to say he agrees, perhaps just out of helplessness. Why did you come south? says the rope. It's scorching, I can't stand this. You're a bedbug, says Gao Hong. You're nothing at all. You're a bloodsucker, aren't you? Sucking me dry. You've accomplished nothing. What do you know about the good things of this world? You think you're a part of the world, you fucking idiot, you think you have a quiet life with everything you need, when actually you're a rat in a sewer! Minglei says nothing. Gao Hong's lips are moving very quickly, as if someone's tugging at her tongue with chopsticks. I'm sorry, says the rope, I can't hold back any longer. It slithers swiftly up Gao Hong's legs and twists around her throat. She tries to speak but can't get a word out. Frantically she tries to shove her fingers between the rope and her neck, but it is ice cold and doesn't give an inch. Her eyes widen as she dies, her injured leg stretches straight out, the bandages unravelling, the broken bone knitting together in an instant. She seems to abruptly recognize the world she is about to leave and her eyelids drift shut, blocking it out. The rope drags her corpse into the envelope. Did she forget? it asks before diving in. She's just like me, nothing more than a letter.

Minglei says nothing because Gao Hong told him to shut up. He gets some tape from his bag and seals the envelope shut, then puts all the letters back into his rucksack. He puts on a baseball cap before leaving the room. Dawn is breaking, and workers are out in the centre of the road wiping the traffic barriers clean. His bag feels a little heavier, but maybe he's just imagining it. I've done everything I can to deal with the past and the present, he tells himself. Yet nothing's changed. I'm still the same, all by myself, my self, just like everyone else. He loathes his job, but he needs it to fill his life. He hails a taxi. The driver doesn't say a word to him. It's always this way, he thinks – if only those two drivers could have swapped places. His rucksack rests on his thighs and he stares straight ahead. Light creeps across the sky like flame across an envelope. As he often does when he has nothing better to do, he silently recites the final letter, which he knows by heart:

Hello Wei Minglei.

It's been a year since you left this place and we've lost touch, but I'm writing to you now. I've made a decision about the thing we talked about. Our secret. If you ask me for a reason I couldn't give you one. You're losing me, but in a way I've slipped into the vast sphere of the universe, so perhaps I'll be a part of whatever you encounter in the future. Let's say you go to Mars – you might find my shoes there. (Let's be bold and imagine humans reach Mars during your lifetime.) The rope is ready for me. I twisted my ankle testing it, but that's fine, I can climb up the chair with one leg. This is my only suicide note, I hope that makes you feel good about yourself. Goodbye, Wei Minglei. I wish you well. Always be as you are now, with nothing between you and your true nature.

Respectfully yours (the only time
I'll copy your sign-off),
Gao Hong

Squirrels

I HAD A FRIEND CALLED FRIDAY – NOT SURE what his real name was, he was more a friend of a friend, someone I got to know at a drinking session. Turned out he and I had graduated from the same high school. We were in the same year but not the same class, so we didn't actually know each other back then, which tells you we were both unpopular in high school, mere bit players. We ran into each other again at a bar a while later and ended up sitting together. He didn't talk much but he was a good drinker, better than me. I could keep up, though – it's not like I was under the table after three rounds. From then on, whenever we both happened to be at that bar on our own, we'd drink together – no pressure, and no pauses either, just solid drinking until closing time.

The bar was between our homes, walking distance for both of us. Plain decor, excellent music.

The owner, a German, was there every day, standing at the counter with a mug of beer in his hand,
spouting atrocious Mandarin: How are you? I am
good! Beer is good! Cheers. Fuck it. We usually sat
at a small table not far from the counter. Friday
appeared to be a regular, or maybe he had a stake in
the place – anyway, the table was always reserved for
him, a candle floating in a dish of water like the little
boat in that essay by Zhang Dai. Our conversation
meandered, sometimes touching on the present, but
mostly we circled around our high school years. For
whatever reason, both of us enjoyed hearing stories
from that time: the setting was familiar because we
both went to the same school, but the anecdotes felt
fresh given we were in different classes – the perfect
degree of familiarity. He was some kind of busi-
nessman, and always wore expensive, well-tailored
clothes and an exquisite wristwatch. I don't know
what he actually did. Being a writer, I sometimes
went a long while without speaking, just clinked
glasses with him, sighed, and listened to the music.
Occasionally a woman would come by and ask,
Anyone sitting here? Friday would usually say, Yes,
we have five friends coming. You could just say no,
I told him once. Why lie? All we ever do is deceive
one another, he said. If we let her sit down, how

many lies do you think she'd tell us? He had a point, I thought. If you take the dimmest possible view of people you'll never be disappointed.

One time, after we'd been drinking for a while, he said, Did you go to Martyrs' Park in junior high?

I thought about it: Yes, in Year Two I think.

– Right. We were probably there at the same time. After two hours of walking, a couple of the girls in my class got heatstroke.

– Yeah, it wasn't just the girls – I almost didn't make it either. My mother gave me a bottle of water but I finished it in the first twenty minutes, then all I could do was watch other people drink. Half an hour in and I was seeing things. I hadn't realized you were there too.

– Remember someone in Class Seven called Ma Liye?

I moved my chair.

– You know her?

– I'm asking if *you* remember her.

– Yeah. She was mixed-race, right? By Year Two she was already like 170 centimetres – black hair, blue eyes.

– Green eyes. Someone told me her ma was Russian.

– Do women's eyes change colour?

– Maybe they do, but hers didn't. They were green and deep-set.

– Fine. They were green if you say so.

– For a while I would go over to her classroom during break and stare at her.

– That I never did.

– I even went to the library to try to teach myself Russian.

At this I glanced over at him. He looked placid, not at all like he was exaggerating. I followed her all the way home and saw her ma, she was definitely foreign, he said, but she spoke Chinese, so I learned all that Russian for nothing.

– Knowledge is never a bad thing. It seems you put a lot of effort into that.

He held up his hand and ordered himself another whiskey. Nothing for me thanks, I said. He nodded.

– I wasn't doing so well at school. My family's ordinary – my mother was a vegetable seller, did you know that?

– You never mentioned it.

– Well, I thought about the situation for a while, and I realized there was only one option – I had to take her by force.

– Wait, what?

So I got hold of some rope and a hammer, Friday

said, as if he hadn't heard me, Then I stole a bottle of ether from my chemistry teacher. All these things sat at the bottom of my schoolbag day after day.

I glanced up at the German guy, wondering if he was hearing any of this. He was talking to a Chinese woman who shrunk in her neck whenever she laughed, like a mole.

I followed Ma Liye for a month, Friday continued, but I never had an opportunity to take her. Her ma always met her at the hutong entrance, and she didn't step out again once she'd reached home. Their apartment windows weren't very secure, so one night I climbed up to the second floor. There was no sign of her ba, but she and her ma slept in the same bed, so that was a no go. I'd have to get past her ma first, but she was a grown-up and I wouldn't have been able to beat her in a fight, and even if I could, Ma Liye wouldn't just sit there and watch, and she was taller than me. Let's say I did manage to subdue them both, all it would take was one scream from either of them and all their neighbours in that crappy tenement building would come swarming in. He raised his hand to call for another drink, ignoring my unease, and grinned. Don't worry, he said, tonight's on me.

I didn't bring the stuff the day we went to Martyrs'

Park, he said, because number one I'd never been there and didn't know the terrain, and number two it was broad daylight, and with three or four hundred people around, anything I did might as well be on a live broadcast. Like you said, it was blazing hot that day, fire pouring down from the sky, and after we'd been walking for a while I felt as if my soles were melting and sticking to the ground. I hadn't been chosen as part of the delegation – my teacher looked down on me, and anyway each class could only send seven or eight people, though it could have been twice as many and she still wouldn't have picked me. It's not like I caused trouble in class. I never said much, and my marks weren't near the bottom or anything, she just looked down on me for whatever weird reason. Or who knows, maybe she *was* a great judge of character and I ought to have been selling vegetables. Anyway, you'll remember that Ma Liye was one of the oath-takers. Oh, you forgot? It was always a guy and a girl, the guy was Cui Lei from our class, you ought to remember him – tall and good-looking, played in the band? And she was the girl. A single path led from the entrance of Martyrs' Park, pine trees on either side, wide enough for a row of ten. We lined up, Class One to Class Eleven. Directly ahead was a memorial, human height, like a mud wall with some commander's name up top and a few other words. The park commemorated martyrs in the War to Support Korea Against the USA, remember? All these people died in Korea, and first they were buried out there, then they were dug up and brought back here. That's what the inscription said, these corpses were brought back in whatever year, and it took so much effort, and their deaths were so worthwhile. The pair of them stood before this memorial and led the oath-taking. Everyone said the same words, first Cui Lei, then Ma Liye, then the rest of the delegation. Those of us who hadn't made it into the delegation stood at the back and listened. We were the audience. We were there to be educated. I was in the second-to-last row and there wasn't even a whisper of breeze, the pine needles by my side weren't moving at all. Ma Liye and Cui Lei were standing in full sunlight. My eyesight was better back then, and even though they were far away I could see Ma Liye's hair sticking to her forehead, the damp patches beneath the short sleeves of the blouse of her uniform, her wide eyes, her straight back, her fist by her temple in salute as she recited, 'I am willing to join the Chinese Communist Youth . . .' Cui Lei must have been around her height, but he'd worn leather shoes with a bit of a heel so he'd look slightly taller. He seemed nervous, even more so than her – his lower lip stuck out and he kept blowing at his centre-parted fringe. A cloud drifted by, providing a bit of shade, a respite. As the oath ended the cloud moved on. The two of them stepped off the platform and took their places in the front row, then the principal made a speech. When he was done, he announced that we were free to explore the park on our own, and we'd meet back in the same place in an hour and a half.

There was a guy in our class we called Monkey, maybe you remember him? Monkey was standing next to me – he hadn't gotten into the delegation either. He produced this air rifle from his bag and said, Come on, let's go hunt squirrels. I looked around. Ma Liye was nowhere to be seen, Cui Lei was talking to our teacher, who handed him a bottle of water and pointed at his collar, which he loosened as he drank. Monkey said, Are you coming? Let's go, I said. We'll head deeper into the park, he said, there are too many people here, they've scared off the squirrels. I followed him between the pine trees and we forged ahead, past the platform where Ma Liye had been standing. Further on we saw a couple of people sitting against the trees, having a drink and eating buns – we kept going till we could see no one at all. Monkey's air rifle was pretty good, looked like it was made of plastic but the tube inside was steel, his father must have modified it for him. It shot these solid plastic bullets that could smash thin glass at twenty metres. We must have walked for ten minutes when a gigantic squirrel scurried past. Monkey's arm jerked up and he fired, hitting the squirrel's tail. A sharp, thin noise came from the animal's throat as its tail drooped, and it began weaving to and fro like it was drunk. Monkey slowly moved closer, and the creature got so agitated all it could do was spin in circles. He turned to me and said, You grab it. Before I could respond, the squirrel leaped over Monkey's feet and shot up a tree trunk like a rocket, vanishing before our eyes. Monkey quickly fired a round at the crown of the tree but that did no good at all, nothing fell down. He shook his head and said, I should have shot it again to make sure. Never mind, there'll be more.

Monkey's ba was a foundry worker with arms that curved like brackets around his torso. I often saw him walking past our home, looking like a baboon. Monkey on the other hand was scrawny and small, hence the nickname. The two of us kept going, but there weren't any squirrels, just dried-out pine-cones. The trees got taller, the sun less scorching.

My sheen of sweat gradually dried, leaving my face feeling like I'd had a saltwater soak. My skin was taut whenever I moved my mouth. Monkey's air rifle was about half a metre long, he kept it clamped under his arm, kicking aside branches as he went to see if he could startle any squirrels. Then out of nowhere we saw a stone arch in front of us, twice the height of a person, standing alone among the trees with no walls to either side. The words 'Unknown Martyrs' Graveyard' were painted in thick black words across it, no date. We went through the archway and found a graveyard, easily a couple of hundred identical tombstones that all said 'Unknown Martyr' with no birth or death years. Same handwriting as the arch. Some had fresh flowers or fruit in front of them, others nothing but withered leaves. We should head back, I said to Monkey. He glanced at his watch. We still have forty minutes, let's leave in ten. I heard leaves rustling further back among the graves and poked Monkey. He held his breath for a few seconds, listening. Don't startle it, he said. We crept forward. I spotted a sneaker poking out from one of the graves. I shoved Monkey and we approached from the side.

The first thing we saw was Ma Liye with her back arched over the grave, then Cui Lei standing in front of her, collar splayed, sweat pouring down his face, still blowing at his fringe. He was staring at her. Her blouse was open, revealing her white bra. Her belly rose and fell as she breathed. Take it off, Cui Lei said. No, we agreed, said Ma Liye. This is all you get to see. Then let me touch them, he said. No, she said. I'm still thinking about it. Through your bra then, he said. No way. Let's head back, she said. Let me touch them and I'll give you a Discman, he said. How dare you? she snapped. I have a Sony I've been passing around the class, he said, I'll give it to you when we get back. My ma will ask where I got it, she said. It's old, can't you just say you found it? he asked. I don't have any CDs, she said. What would I do with a Discman? I have dozens, he said, you can choose any five you like.

Monkey turned and whispered to me, Cui Lei sure is generous. I reached out my hand, Give me the gun. What for? he said. I saw a squirrel, I said. Where? Quick, it's getting away, I said. Lifting the rifle, I was about to fire when a finger reached out and blocked the trigger. I turned and saw a man in army uniform crouching, staring straight at me. Monkey looked startled too. What do you want? he said. The guy was about twenty, no hat, crew cut, face full of acne, short and well-built. If he'd been a bit older I'd have guessed he was the caretaker. He had puttees wrapped around his legs, a military green water canteen strapped across his chest, and a soft hat tucked into his belt. It's hot, are you staying hydrated? he asked. We shook our heads. The heat doesn't matter, he said. It affects the enemy and us the same way. He gestured at Ma Liye, who was reaching behind her to unclasp her bra, and said, Are you with them? We're schoolmates, Monkey said, we were about to go call them, it's almost time to assemble. The soldier smiled. That's not what it looks like. Aren't the pair of you just watching? What's with the crappy rifle, anyway? Panicking, I thrust the air rifle back at Monkey and said, It's not mine. Don't stress, he said. I know what you want to do, but come on, what kind of place is this? Making out here seems kind of inappropriate, and the woman looks like a foreigner. She American? I wanted to say that she might look foreign but she was actually Chinese, but I held my tongue. Yes, Monkey said, yes it's inappropriate, I'll tell them to stop. Don't bother, just listen for my command, said the soldier.

With that, he pulled out a couple of handguns from behind his back, placed one in my grip, and held the other up like a conductor's baton. Pointing it at me, he said, Shoot them. It took me both hands to lift the gun, which was so old the black had rubbed off the barrel and the steel was showing through. It was ice cold. I suddenly remembered my catchphrase and blurted out, I was wrong – I know it was my fault. He held his gun to my head and said, Shoot the boy first, he'll fall on top of her so she won't be able to get away. He'll run if you shoot her first, and a moving target is harder to hit. Monkey was petrified, not even able to scream, eyes fixed on the guns in our hands. The soldier said, I'll count to three, and you'll fire. I need to pee, I said. Can't you see we're in school uniform? said Monkey. We don't know anything, we couldn't even hit a squirrel. The soldier said to me, I need you to do a commando crawl. Do you know what that is? Great, I'll start counting. That's when Ma Liye's hands stopped moving and she said, I can't reach. Cui Lei said, I'll do it for you. Let's head back, she said. Let me do it, he said. Ma Liye started buttoning up her blouse and said, You can keep your Discman. Cui Lei grabbed her arm. How can you change your mind just like that? What do you think? she said. This just feels so shameless. Cui Lei scooted over so that his legs were pressed against hers, and he nibbled at her ear. Without waiting for the man to start counting, I pulled the trigger. Cui Lei cried out and slumped forward, pinning Ma Liye to the ground. Monkey shrieked and sprinted away.

The man with the puttees patted me on the shoulder and said, Good stuff, young man. He took the gun back from me and stuck it in his belt, then stuffed an apple into my trouser pocket. Eat this, he said. It was shipped in by air. Can't have been cheap – wrenched from the mouths of the people. Remember: next time you fire a gun, keep your eyes open. He stood and walked away.

I shut my eyes for a moment before I went over to Ma Liye, but I stumbled on my first step, split my lip open, and had to crawl the rest of the way. Ma Liye was still on the ground. She had flipped Cui Lei over and was pawing at his midsection. Come quick, she called when she saw me. Cui Lei's eyes were shut and his legs were ramrod straight. He's got heatstroke, do you have any water? No, I said. Which class are you in? she asked. Class Nine. She nodded, her green eyes dazzling. I have an apple, I said. Hand it over. She took it, smashed it on the ground and smeared the juice over Cui Lei's lips. He revived, then stared at Ma Liye and me, unable to work out what had happened. Ma Liye smacked him in the face and said, If you ever come near me again, I'll kill you. Cui Lei blinked by way of saying yes. She slapped him again and said, How do you feel? Better, he said, much better. We walked back with him slung between us, all the way to the assembly point where everyone was gathering. Cui Lei reeked sweetly of apple. We were just in time.

By now my beer had grown warm. What happened to Monkey? I said. Let me see, I think he ran all the way home, said Friday. I remember him, I said. He got tall later, but stayed stupid. Yeah, no one knows how tall they're going to grow, he said. The bar was filling up – people were watching the game, chattering about it in English, occasionally letting out a roar. I might turn this into a short story, I said. What are you going to call me? he said. No idea. Just make it something good, he said. What's today? I asked. Friday, he said. Start of the weekend. When we were kids, the weekend started on Saturday, I said. True, he said. Maybe in another decade the weekend will start with Thursday. I'll call you Friday then, I said. He thought about it and said, Sure. But wasn't there someone with that name in *Robinson Crusoe*? I don't care about that, I said. Don't be so picky, first thought best thought. Fine, he said. Then he stood up and paid the bill, and when he was done he didn't come back to the table or look back at me, he just walked briskly out of the bar.

Martial Artist

DOU DOU WAS FIFTEEN WHEN HIS FATHER DIED.
Before then it had never crossed his mind that this
was a possibility. His father, Dou Chongshi, was
the head of the Fengtian Five Loves Martial Arts
Institute. At ten in the morning on 22 December
1932 he sat in the hall of the institute waiting for the
Japanese martial artist Hashimoto Toshiro, who had
been living in northeast China for many years, even
before the Japanese occupation, and who made a
living taking part in boxing matches. Hashimoto had
gotten into martial arts via kendo, and practised a
form of left-leaning boxing with twenty-four stances.
In the ring he looked like he was having a stroke:
one leg dragged behind the other, every movement
was twisted, and his hands trailed from droopy arms
towards the ground. He remained undefeated. His
right arm was his sword, leading the charge. His left
arm wrapped itself around your ankle and jerked to

the left while his shoulder shoved into your knee, and next thing you knew he'd be standing on your back. Chinese martial arts masters called him Lefty. Lefty wasn't considered a leftist in Japan, nor did he lean to the right. He lacked a military background and wasn't in any of the folk organizations loyal to the Emperor. He was simply an internationalist. He'd come to China for no other reason than to fight.

It had snowed a little the night before, and two servants were slowly clearing the ground with wide brooms. Dou Chongshi added hot water to the teapot and watched the scene before him with a twinge of loneliness. His wife, Dou Dou's mother, had died young, but he had never remarried. He didn't have the time, and besides, there were fewer and fewer people he could trust.

Almost no one knew Mr Dou was a Communist Party member. Even his closest friends only knew him as an exceptionally talented pugilist who'd been training virtually since birth. After establishing his own school of fighting at an early age, he'd set up the institute and began taking in disciples. Someday his funeral hall would surely be piled high with floral tributes from all manner of people. Dou Chongshi practised a combination of Bagua fighting and

Manchu wrestling. The Bagua fighting he'd inherited from his father, and his mother, who was Manchu, taught him a rhyming sequence she'd memorized that, once deciphered, allowed him to master the wrestling moves. His fists absorbed this unique fighting style. As a result, he led off his Bagua stance with downturned hands, contrasting with the skyward-facing palms of other practitioners. His version of Bagua style involved sinuously entwining his opponents' limbs, grabbing at their clothes and tripping them over, making it impossible for them to disentangle themselves. He'd acquired the childhood nickname Sticky Burr, from an old Fengtian saying, but as his reputation spread to Beiping he managed to shake off this tag and go by 'Mr Dou'.

Dou Chongshi had never met Lefty before, though they'd exchanged letters about martial arts. Nothing personal, strictly business. Mr Dou hated the Japanese, every last one of them: good or bad, old or young. He'd seen their vile actions with his own eyes, of course, but he also detested uninvited guests. He knew he couldn't beat them on his own, so he kept his loathing buried deep. He understood Japanese martial arts very well – as the saying goes, know yourself well and know your enemy better – but whenever a Japanese person showed up wanting a bout, he received them politely, served them tea, then refused their offer. Win or lose, he knew he'd come out looking bad.

Secretly, Dou Chongshi was providing the Party with space for meetings. He also trained assassins for them, though he never carried out hits himself – he had a child to think of. His enmity for the Japanese was strictly nationalistic. It wasn't a family vendetta, so why put his life on the line? He was too canny for that. During their correspondence, he had learned that Lefty possessed a high level of martial arts skills in addition to being well educated. During his years in China, Lefty had maintained a good reputation: he showed mercy when necessary and never fatally injured anyone – he was just a martial arts obsessive. Still, Mr Dou never shared his insights about fighting in any of his letters to Lefty. He aired his views about everything from the philosophy of Mencius to the movement aimed at overturning the Qing and restoring the Ming, from pugilist gossip to the intersection of Confucianism and Buddhism, but he never wrote a single word about the deeper truths of martial arts. On this morning he laid out tea and snacks, and prepared a gift hamper of tradition-ally smoked chicken. Now he sat in the master's seat in the main hall, awaiting Lefty. Behind him were

calligraphic scrolls he'd written himself: Chongdan
– seek peace – on the left, Budou – not conflict – on
the right, containing characters taken from his and
his son's names, although in fact the 'Dou' in Dou
Dou's given name was pronounced with a rising
tone and meant 'dipper' – because a single dipperful
of martial arts training was all he needed.

Lefty arrived at ten, as arranged. He brought with
him a boy of fifteen or sixteen: shaved head, very
skinny, wearing only a pale grey robe even though
it was the middle of winter. Dou Chongshi was
momentarily thrown – he'd expected Lefty to come
alone. Lefty wore a deep blue Chinese-style padded
jacket that revealed a slight pot belly, along with a
fox-pelt scarf and long black leather boots with a
white fleece lining. At a glance he looked exactly like
a prosperous Chinese elder. After some small talk,
Lefty said in his precise Mandarin, Mr Dou, I have
heard that you do not duel with Japanese people,
and I deeply empathize with your reasons for this.
You have led me in circles with your letters, and this
I understand too. I have come today not to ask for
a fight, but for something else: I have heard that in
your possession is a Yamakage Ittō-ryū sword manual, something that belongs to my family, and I'm
here to retrieve it. You are making fun of me, sir,

said Dou Chongshi. I'm an ordinary Chinese pugi-list, why would I possibly have a Japanese sword manual? Major Fujino died five days ago in a hutong near South Market, said Lefty. He was once my disciple, an unworthy man, and he stole the sword manual from me. I could do nothing while he remained in the army. The manual documents an evil art: those who master it may generate a shadow self of the opposite gender. This shadow self has form but no substance, and it draws no breath. In combat, the fighter and his shadow self can ambush their opponents. With every person it kills, the shadow self gains a little of its owner's essence, and when the owner dies the shadow self wanders the world alone, undetectable. This art is known as Yi, shifting. Our ancestors did not allow us to prac-tise it, but we held on to the manual – such an exquisite piece of work that no one could bear to destroy it. I know that you, my brother, have had secret dealings with the Communist Party, and Fuji-no's death must have had something to do with you, but that's not important. People will do what they will. But as a descendant of the Yamakage Ittō-ryū, it is my duty to retrieve the manual. In exchange, I can offer you three hundred jin of valuable medi-cinal herbs, to do with as you please. They're waiting outside your front door – you just need to give the word.

Dou Chongshi took a short time to think about this. Rarely in his life had he been forced to concentrate so intently, but he knew this was an important decision. He did indeed have the manual, and although he'd glanced at the illustrations, the method was written in Japanese, and so was incomprehensible to him. It had never crossed his mind that this might be an important book – he'd assumed it was merely loot, something a disciple had lifted from a corpse. Fortunately, it did not sound like Fujino had studied the method either. The man before him seemed candid and transparent. The manual was a family heirloom, and for that reason it ought to be returned – but then, Lefty was Japanese. What if he had a change of heart someday and handed it over to a Japanese kamikaze unit or ninja squad? Their victims would almost certainly be Chinese. Besides, if he admitted to having the manual, he'd have to reveal his connection to the Party, which was unthinkable. And so Dou Chongshi said, Respected sir, everything you've said sounds to me like a tale out of the Arabian Nights. I have been training in martial arts all my life to strengthen my body, to be in harmony with the heavens and earth, but I have never heard of this Yi you mention. Nor have I come across such a manual. I'm an ordinary citizen with no interest in politics, and I am in no way connected to the Communist Party – whenever a new disciple joins us, the first thing I teach them is that we belong to no parties and no sects. Rumours must fall when faced with a learned man. Your fairy tale will have to end here, respected sir.

As Dou Chongshi finished speaking and signalled for the servants to serve tea, the boy sitting to Lefty's right suddenly sprang to his feet. He took a couple of bounds and grabbed Mr Dou by the lapels. Hand it over! he said. Dou Chongshi had spent twenty years traversing the dangerous Shanhai Pass, but he'd never been manhandled like this. The speed of the attack was like a bullet. Remaining calm, he shoved the boy's armpits rather than catching hold of his wrists and said, Have some tea, young man. The boy vaulted backwards twenty feet and produced two knives from behind his back, each about a foot long and two inches wide. He struck them together. Give it here! Dou Chongshi stood and said, I truly don't have it. The boy attacked again, but this time Dou Chongshi was prepared. He dodged the knife in the boy's left hand while reaching out with both palms face down to grab the attacker's wrist. With his Bagua skills, if he managed to grab hold of his opponent's clothing, it would be near impossible to shake him off. Don't make an enemy when there is no need! Lefty shouted. Out of nowhere, a young woman flashed into existence next to the boy – the same height, dressed in a red robe, with her hair in two buns, wielding the same twin blades. She lunged at Dou Chongshi. Could this actually be black magic? He tried to retreat, but the youth had already manoeuvred his way behind his back and lopped off his head with a single blow. Gurgling with laughter, the woman kicked the severed head out into the courtyard, where it landed in a snowdrift.

By the time Dou Dou arrived home, his father was dead and the murderers were long gone. An old servant lost his life trying to stop them from fleeing, two stab wounds straight through his heart. The bundle of medicinal herbs still stood by the gate, but they couldn't save anyone's life now. The household swiftly crumbled. Dou Dou was an only child, and now that both his parents were dead their possessions would be divided among several older relatives. One uncle kindly gave Dou Dou a gold ingot so that he could make his way in the world. Dou Dou had learnt some martial arts as a young boy, but he had never really been that interested.

His passion was for books, and Dou Chongshi always respected this choice. After all, there were plenty of disciples who could take over the teaching, and the world of martial arts was a dangerous one. Besides, the New Society was evolving in a different direction. A servant who'd witnessed the fight had overheard the conversation about the manual, though his testimony was confused – he referred first to there being two visitors, then to three. When Dou Chongshi's possessions were auctioned off, the sword manual was not found among his books. His study looked like it had been ransacked – probably the intruders had made off with it. Dou Dou weighed up his prospects and decided that there was little point remaining in Fengtian. He no longer had a home, so it didn't matter where he went. Before the mourning period was over, he packed his bags and took the train to Beiping. There were quite a few universities there, and he hoped to find a work–study programme that would support him with his education. He'd only made it as far as high school in Fengtian, but if he worked hard he might yet pass the entrance exam.

He bought a roast yam on the platform at Beiping station. Yams are so much sweeter in the winter. He bought a second one as soon as he finished the first. He thought of his mother. His memories of her were hazy, just her holding up his dinner in a large patterned bowl. His father was busy all his life, either fighting or bent over his desk, and Dou Dou never dared disturb him. He couldn't recollect ever seeking him out – mostly it was his father who called him over to ask how his studies were going, or to give him words of advice which he generally could have thought of himself.

As he walked towards the station exit, a man in a top hat bumped him with a newspaper and he dropped his yam. Pardon me, said the man. Dou Dou hunched over, not daring to answer. What are you doing in Beiping? said the man. Studying, said Dou Dou quietly. Oh, said the man, you're not here for revenge? Shaken, Dou Dou looked up at the man's face: moustache, square jaw, vertical scar over the right eyebrow. Mr Dou was our comrade, said the man. We didn't pay our respects at his wake because we did not wish to cause you trouble. A thousand apologies. Dou Dou hurried away muttering, It's fine, it's fine. The man grabbed his arm, Hold on, he said. We bear a little responsibility for Mr Dou's death, so here's a small token. He produced two bags of silver dollars from his pocket and pressed them into Dou Dou's hand. I can't accept this, said

Dou Dou. I don't know you. I worked alongside your father for many years, said the man. I had a lot of respect for his skills as a martial artist, and even though he wasn't a true believer he made solid practical contributions to our cause. As for the question of revenge, we've had a meeting and decided it must happen no matter how arduous the process, so you don't need to worry about anything. I don't want revenge, said Dou Dou. What you do is your own business. Why not? asked the man. That's what our family decided, said Dou Dou. First, because my father's opponent didn't win through force of numbers. If a single person beats you to death, according to the rules of combat, there's nothing to be done. Second, I don't know martial arts, and even if I did I wouldn't be able to defeat anyone. My father was killed, and I would be too, even if I trained for thirty years. He paused for a moment. There are other things I wish to pursue, he said, rather than spending a lifetime on this. What things? asked the man. I'm not sure yet, said Dou Dou. I came to Beiping to think that through. We won't press you, said the man, but because his killer was Japanese, we need to take revenge. Even if he flees back to Japan we'll follow him. The man pulled a stitch-bound book from his jacket and said, This is for you. You keep giving me things I don't want, said Dou Dou. The Japanese man visited your father that day looking for this very sword manual, said the man. We've talked it over, and decided it should be returned to you. Wait, why do you have it? asked Dou Dou. Your family servant, the only witness, was one of our people, said the man. Your father had no idea. When the fighting started, the servant hid the manual. Old Jin was yours? said Dou Dou. Yes, said the man. He was with your family for a decade, and the whole time he was working for us. Your father died for this manual, now you must take it. Wouldn't it be more use to you? asked Dou Dou. Have another meeting. We don't need to, said the man. After seeing what happened to your father, we'll be relying on guns from now on. Before Dou Dou could say any more, the man had pressed the silver dollars and manual on him, and was striding away.

Dou Dou found lodgings at an inn next to Peking University. With his gold ingot and silver dollars, he'd be able to support himself for more than a year. He realized as he paid the innkeeper how useful these silver dollars were going to be. Beiping was much more expensive than Fengtian – even a light bulb cost twice as much here. He thought fondly of the square-jawed man. Truly a good comrade to his father. It was 1933, just after Lunar New Year. Peking U was still on winter break so there weren't many students around. Dou Dou wandered through the campus and found it huge, like an enormous park. He spent three weeks reading in the mornings and browsing used bookstores in the afternoons. When the weather was good, he rode his bicycle around the hutong alleyways. The Forbidden City held no emperor, and the presidential palace no longer contained warlords. Generalissimo Chiang had set up his lair in Nanjing, leaving Beiping a place of culture. Dou Dou read in the papers that Japanese forces had broken through the Shanhai Pass, and in a burst of terror he wondered if they had come in pursuit of him. The next day, the papers reported that General Fu Zuoyi had proclaimed that the Japanese would not advance one step further. His forces had staked out the Great Wall with German-manufactured machine guns, so residents of Beiping should rest easy. This reminded Dou Dou that he hadn't yet seen the Great Wall, though this was clearly not the moment for that.

After the winter holidays, classes started again and the campus filled up with students, clean-cut young men and women fresh as a spring breeze. Dou Dou realized that Beipingers had no idea what the

Japanese were capable of and had never imagined falling into the hands of the enemy. Growing up in Fengtian, he'd been forced to learn Japanese. When he encountered a Japanese person in the street, he'd had to stand pressed against the wall to let them pass. Now he bought three newspapers every day to keep up with current events, which made him feel much more mature than the vast majority of Beipingers.

He began auditing classes, hoping to find a suitable profession. After a month of this, he was certain of what he'd only suspected before: his place was in the Chinese department. He wasn't sure what he would do afterwards, but at least he would be a man of culture. One habit of his had remained unchanged since he was a child: practising standing meditation by the lakeside first thing every morning. This was the only thing Dou Chongshi had handed down to him, and he didn't want to lose it. Besides, it left him full of energy, which meant he could study longer without getting tired. Standing meditation wasn't connected to Bagua fighting or Manchu wrestling, but Dou Chongshi had felt that it cultivated the eye and heart, and that it was useful when transforming Bagua moves into pillar stances. Dou Dou never opened the sword manual. It remained locked away in a cabinet, wrapped in one of his leather jackets. It seemed clear to him that there would soon be no such thing as a martial artist, which meant his current existence and his previous life at home belonged to two completely different eras. His professors mostly talked about democracy and science, neither of which martial arts could lay any claim to possessing.

Meals were provided at the inn, but because he had a bit of spare cash, Dou Dou sometimes sought out tastier food. One night he enjoyed a tray of steamed dumplings and a couple of meat pies at a nearby restaurant. As he wandered back to the inn, he saw a crowd gathered around a young woman who was running through a martial arts routine. She was dressed all in red, her hair in two buns secured with scarlet ribbons, and only her shoes were white, rising into the air like plump snowballs with each high kick. He watched for a while. Even with his limited knowledge, he could tell this was a very basic Six Harmonies sequence, but she was limber enough to make it look beautiful. When she was done, she wiped the sweat from her brow and clasped her hands, saying to the crowd, Thank you, thank you. I didn't come here to ask for money – I'm searching for my brother. He has a long face and big eyes, and usually dresses in blue. We came to Beiping together, then one morning I woke up and he was gone. He's a very skilled double-blade fighter. As she spoke, she produced a pair of daggers from her bag and continued, He uses two knives just like these. He has no other way to earn money, so he's probably doing martial arts displays like me. If you see him, please let me know. I'd be ever so grateful. Seeing that the girl was no longer practising, the crowd dispersed.

Dou Dou lounged in bed reading until around ten, when he put out the lamp and fell asleep. That night he dreamt that his house was on fire and all the servants had fled, abandoning his father. Sobbing, he cried out, Ba, Ba! In a flash of inspiration, Dou Chongshi jumped into the water tank in the courtyard. When the fire had burned itself out, Dou Dou ran to the tank, but his father was gone, leaving only a sheet of paper floating on the surface. These were Dou Chongshi's last words to him: *Remember this: it doesn't matter if you don't make anything of yourself, so long as you eat three meals a day.* Dou Dou remembered that he'd skipped lunch because he had been so absorbed in browsing the antiques at Liulichang market, and the stab of guilt woke him.

A man in his fifties was sitting at Dou Dou's desk, reading a book. Not daring to get out of bed or make a sound, Dou Dou shut his eyes then opened them again. The man was still there. This was no dream. The man noticed his eyes were open and said, Nightmare?

– Who are you?

– It's complicated. To put it simply, I'm your enemy.

– You're Lefty?

– That's right. Where did you get this sword manual?

– I can't tell you.

– I imagine the Communists gave it to you. It's the real thing, not missing one page.

– Go ahead and take it.

Lefty chuckled: That's generous of you. You're not like your father at all. I carried this manual around for twenty years and never once looked at it. Fujino got hold of it but died before he could put it to use. Only my disciple Kin actually studied it, and landed in terrible trouble. So why do you think I'd have any use for it?

Dou Dou was starting to understand. Kin must be the man who killed his father.

– Where is Kin now?

– Gone. That girl you saw yesterday is Kin.

– What are you talking about?

– It's hard to explain. I've been tailing you since you got off the train. The Communists were too – I saw them give you the manual. That was bait. They wanted to lure me out. They have quite a few people stationed around this inn – it wasn't easy for me to get in. To cut a long story short, the young woman is named Kinbai, and she's Kin's shadow. Now that Kin is dead she's become real, but she believes Kin is her big brother. That's why she's been searching for him. It's written on the last page of this manual that these shadows always end up restlessly wandering the world, seeking their true selves. That's why this whole practice is evil.

Lefty sighed long and hard: I've been enraptured by martial arts all my life. I never got wrapped up in the grudges and gratitudes of the world, but now they've become unavoidable, so I can't return to Japan just yet.

– And what about the girl?

– To be honest, I'm not completely sure what kind of thing she is, or whether her suffering counts as true suffering. But there is one thing I do know: no ordinary person can kill her.

– Why not?

– She's a ghost in human form. She just doesn't realize it. The manual does include a method for exterminating her: a Japanese curse. As she sleeps, you have to whisper in her ear *Harusame no ware maboroshi ni chikaki mizo*. In Chinese that means *The spring rain is misty, I pass into illusion*. Once you've said the words, she'll understand her true nature and vanish in a puff of smoke. Young Mr Dou, I didn't mean to kill your father. I'm offering you this phrase as a sign of my goodwill. You can decide what to do with it.

With that, he produced a box of matches and burnt the sword manual, then he pushed open the wooden shutters and leapt outside. A few hurried footsteps and he was gone.

The next day, Dou Dou moved to a different hotel, this time by the east gate of the university. A few days later he read in the paper that the famous Japanese martial artist Hashimoto Toshiro had been shot dead while boarding a boat. He'd instinctively raised his left hand in defence, and the bullet had passed straight through his palm before reaching his heart. The killer had jumped into the sea and escaped.

Dou Dou went on to take the college entrance exam and won himself a place in the Chinese department. Around the time he graduated, the Japanese thundered into Beiping. By the time Tianjin fell he had already left. After some wandering he ended up as an assistant to the poet Wen Yiduo at the National Southwestern Associated University. His main research area was Tang poetry, though his actual work was more like a librarian's: fetching whatever books Mr Wen required, reading the materials Mr Wen didn't have time to look at and preparing digests. Being fluent in Japanese, he was particularly helpful at deciphering Japanese books. When Mr Wen was assassinated, Dou Dou spent the night sobbing, and the next day took over as lecturer. He wasn't much of a speaker, so his classes were poorly attended and the students largely dozed through them. Fortunately, university standards were lax given the confusion of war, and he was able to keep his position. He never married, and never tried to accomplish anything. All he wanted was a peaceful life. Apart from research and teaching, his greatest interest was in standing meditation, which he did for longer and longer periods as he aged, in the morning and at night. After turning forty, he started standing all night long, insisting he slept better that way. When he meditated, everything – avenging his father's murder, Mr Wen's death, the country's troubles – melted away into the earth and sky, and he felt his body vanish. As Zhuangzi says: *One experiences misfortune because one has a self. If the self did not exist, how could one suffer?*

After the founding of the People's Republic, Dou Dou returned to Beijing (no longer Beiping, now the Nationalists were gone) and took up a position at the reconstructed Peking University, still teaching Tang poetry. He escaped attack during the various purges of the Cultural Revolution, largely because his father and his professor had both been martyred, which made his background unimpeachable. He joined no faction and sought no fame. When classes stopped, he stayed home and read, and when they resumed he showed up as his timetable dictated. Quite a few prominent figures were locked up in the cowshed, and sometimes he brought them food. Anyone else would have gotten into trouble for doing that, but seeing it was him no one said anything – his personality was as bland as plain vegetable soup, and he was clearly motivated by pure humanism and absolutely nothing else. In the winter of 1969, notices appeared all over the university: *Seeking a martial artist aged around 50, usually dressed in blue. Eager to fight, uses double daggers. Speaks Chinese with a Japanese accent. Has spent time in the northeast. Last seen around Peking U. If you know anything, please contact the ——— office. Anyone with information they fail to report will be severely punished.* Dou Dou stood in front of one of these posters for a moment, then walked away with his head bowed. The next day, he made some jiaozi dumplings and brought them to the cowshed. As a prominent personage popped a dumpling into his mouth, Dou Dou asked, Have you heard about the notices around the school? The personage drew a breath. Yes, someone's searching for a martial artist. It had a red heading like an official document, said Dou Dou. What does that mean? The personage whispered, I heard it's a powerful woman looking for her brother who's been missing for years. Don't worry about it, we live in turbulent times. Let her search, it keeps her busy. Dou Dou nodded and left with his lunchbox.

Soon the new year arrived. It was announced that the influential woman would be visiting the university for the annual variety show, which was advertised as dedicated to culture and martial arts, even though the latter took up seven-tenths of the programme. Dou Dou applied for tickets, for once making use of his status to push for seats near the front. The school agreed after yet another political screening. On the morning of the show, Dou Dou performed his standing meditation by the lake from dawn till noon. He opened his eyes and stared out into the distance. The name of his hometown had changed from Fengtian to Shenyang, but it remained too far away for him to see. He remembered the sixty-four Bagua stances his father had taught him as a child. No complex variations, just the basic stances. He'd thought they were gone from his mind, but as he started running through the sequence, he found he could remember most of it, skipping the few poses he couldn't recall. It had been forty years since he'd last done this. He was sweating profusely by the time he'd finished. The lack of self that Zhuangzi spoke of was no longer open to him – he could feel his solid body emanating warmth like a hot spring.

The show started at eight. Dou Dou was in the row behind the guest of honour. Her greying hair was in a bob. She sat so upright that her back barely touched her seat – you could tell at a glance she was a martial artist. During a demonstration by a warrior wielding double daggers, Dou Dou heard her murmuring to the school official next to her: This one's no good, his blades stick out from his arms – he hasn't learn to tilt them inwards. The last portion of the show was mostly cultural performances. The woman began to droop, and finally she dozed off during a long operatic section. Dou Dou rose and squeezed past pair after pair of legs until he was directly behind her. Bending over, he whispered, *Harusame no ware maboroshi ni chikaki mizo.* She jerked awake and swung around. I see, she said. I'm done for, you cruel man. With that she vanished in a puff of smoke. The heat of the crowd wafted the smoke into the air, so she hovered for a moment above the stage, and then she was gone.

Hunter

LU DONG MOVES THE STANDING LAMP, TURNS to gauge how far he is from the wall, then goes back to the chair he's carefully positioned – no, never mind the chair, better to be prone on the floor. Pulling open the glass door, he steps out onto the balcony and extends a clothes-drying pole into the open air. Not heavy enough. That's the most pressing problem – not the lamp, not the colour of the floorboards, not the table in his peripheral vision distracting him from his target, but the pole's insufficient weight.

His wife Liu Yiduo and their child are in the bedroom playing with Lego. He hears his daughter say, Mama, I can't read the plan, but I know this wheel is wrong. Lu Fan is four and a half, and can already express herself fairly well. Sometimes she uses startling metaphors. During New Year, when their neighbours were setting off fireworks high into the sky, she said, Look, Baba, the stars are breaking apart. Lu Dong keeps his child's words locked in his heart, a whole string of quotes he's memorized – not to repeat to anyone else, just for himself. He believes Lu Fan is an extraordinary child who will do exceptional work someday, something superlative. She could be an artist, but not just any kind of artist. No, when she's grown, some new form of art will surely emerge – maybe she'll sit among a crowd and spout metaphors, or wear a helmet that allows her to beam the imaginings of her mind directly onto a screen. But this speculation has to be kept under wraps for now, otherwise it'll be like when you lift the lid off a pot of steaming rice too soon and it seizes up, half raw.

Lu Dong is a fifth-rate actor – that's by his own ranking system. The first-rate ones are the big movie stars with burnished reputations who make headlines with every appearance, the ones who earn money as easily as turning on a tap. Second-rate actors are talented enough to support themselves with their craft – they have numerous films or TV series to their names, and they reach deep into the human heart with every role. Third-rate actors are youngish and show potential but haven't been in anything really good yet. People think well of them and, with time, depending on personal development and luck, they might attain the first or second rank. The general public would struggle to name any fourth-rate actors, but their faces are familiar from the many TV shows they appear in, playing roles that leave no impression whatsoever. Their features are like a faded backdrop you know you've seen before, and as soon as they appear on screen you feel a sort of reassurance – that's right, this is the sort of show I've always watched, and here are the people who help me pass the time. So what's a fifth-rate actor? Someone who's been in quite a few shows, but for whatever reason – whether it's down to his lack of skill or his appearance – he might as well not have done any. He's spoken many lines and been featured in many shots, but at the end of the day his screen time vanishes as cleanly as water seeping down into the earth. Then a decade passes and he's still in the profession, never really having been out of work, though he's often just twiddling his thumbs. According to Lu Dong, this sort of actor tends to be once-divorced, and now rents an apartment in an okay location, not too far from where other screen actors live. Sometimes at the supermarket a star he's worked with will be standing in line behind him in a face mask and dark glasses, but these stars never recognize him. He's wanted to turn and say, Hey, remember me? That night shoot five years ago – I carried you through the woods on my back, dodging bursts of gunfire, but just as I managed to sling you onto a pony a bullet got me and I died. So far he's only ever thought these words, paid for his groceries, then left.

It's a Sunday morning in Beijing, and the May air is full of floating willow catkins. Lu Dong hefts the pole in his hand. His heart feels more arid than ever before. Three nights ago he had dinner with his lover, then they headed to her place. Usually he doesn't drink much, just enough to take the edge off, but that night he had more than a glass or two because he was getting tired of her, and vice versa, probably. They both needed new partners. Alcohol loosened his tongue, and he began bragging about how he'd always get to the highest point when they played climb-the-flagpole in high school. He'd shimmy down with his legs clamped tight around the slippery pole, pleasurable in a way he couldn't describe. He never got all the way up to the red flag, even though he was at his strongest then – his legs would always give out a couple of metres from the flag and he'd slide back down. One time it was snowing and he climbed towards the falling flakes, wearing gloves and kneepads, and he almost made it – his hand was reaching out to where the flag met the pole when a girl down below tugged at the rope and sent it flicking out to hit him in the eye. He lost his grip and fell. Broke his arm. Swiping at her phone, his lover asked if he could spend the night, but he said no, which brought an end to their nostalgia-tinged drinking session.

On the way home, the night breeze carried a vegetal scent. Outside a nightclub a man sat on the kerb smoking, looking remarkably sober. The man glanced at Lu Dong's face, then lowered his head again. A few seconds later, the man called out, Hey, where do I know you from? Lu Dong had recognized him: Zhang Yu, a well-known director of arthouse films. Fifteen years ago, he'd made a small film with a budget of three hundred grand with Lu Dong as the second lead, a contract killer who kept losing his wallet, a role for which he was paid five thousand yuan. Lu Dong hadn't put on much weight since then, though his face was now fleshier, mostly pouching beneath his eyes and on his jowls. The eyelashes that Zhang Yu had hired him for were still as resplendent as ever, reaching out like a pair of quotation marks, though the eyes they framed looked smaller thanks to the pouching. It's me, Lu

Dong, he said. I was in one of your films. Oh right, said Zhang Yu, I remember. Come, sit. Cigarette? Lu Dong smoked two packs a day so he sat down and took the proffered cigarette. It was rather mild, but the tobacco seemed to become a giant finger inside his lungs, and his face went red right away.

It was too noisy inside, Zhang Yu said, and they're all drunk. I doubt anyone even noticed me leave. Lu Dong nodded. Zhang Yu might have won a Golden Bear and a Silver Lion, but he seemed the same as before – whether on set or in his private life, as soon as a situation bored him he'd go off on his own. He seems as shy as ever, Lu Dong thought, and just like before he gets embarrassed for other people, which causes him unnecessary pain. What are you busy with? Zhang Yu asked. Running around, Lu Dong said, taking on whatever roles I can. You married? Yes, said Lu Dong. My daughter's four. That's good, said Zhang Yu, I've been divorced twice in the last decade. The second time was like a photocopy of the first – I remember back in the day you weren't in favour of me getting married, but I didn't listen. Turns out you were right. You're a good actor, you know, it's just that you don't fit in and there's nothing special about your looks. But the real problem is that your desire is low and your boiling point is high. With successful actors it's the other way round.

Lu Dong nodded and said nothing. He was well aware of where he stood, but he loved acting. That's not the sort of thing you say out loud. True, he'd persisted till now out of love for the craft, but when you say something like that it sounds fake. Zhang Yu shook another cigarette from the pack, tapped it on his knee and said, Walk a few paces. Lu Dong stood and did as he was asked. Go a little further, Zhang Yu said, up to that streetlight. Lu Dong kept going, suddenly realizing he ought to walk properly, as if a voice from very far away was saying, I'm begging you, take this seriously. A tender voice. Motherly, pleading. As he walked he loosened his belt, and when he reached the streetlight, he let loose a stream of piss that he'd been holding in for some time. Then he fastened his trousers and came back.

Zhang Yu indicated for him to sit again. Come be in my new film, he said. It's a supporting role, but there's nothing run-of-the-mill about it, a colourful part, you know what I mean? Lu Dong's belly churned and he thought he might need to shit. Sure, he said. Thank you, Director Zhang. What's your usual fee? Zhang Yu asked. I'm very cheap, Lu Dong said, just pay me whatever you think. Let's go with a round number, a hundred grand, Zhang Yu said. I know that's not a lot – maybe it's not commensurate with your ability. I hope you don't mind. It's a three-month shoot in Xi'an, starting two months from now. You won't need to learn Shaanxi dialect, we'll film in Mandarin. I'm still working with the same crew. You've met most of them. They're still in there, singing karaoke. Come back inside with me in a moment and I'll re-introduce you. They've gotten older just like I have, as you'd expect. The script is adapted from a story by a Xi'an author, Han Chun. I'll send you a copy tomorrow, along with a contract. You'll be playing a killer again – a sharpshooter. You like noodles? I can't remember. Frankly my digestion isn't great, said Lu Dong, so I'm always eating noodles. Good, said Zhang Yu, go learn to cook noodles. You'll need to have a relationship with noodles as well as with your rifle. This character treats shooting as a very serious business – like they say, 'Where the focus lies, there you'll find the spirit.' Know what I mean? I'll start practising, said Lu Dong. I don't need you to practise, said Zhang Yu. I need you to become the character. And you'll need to lose a bit of weight off your face too.

The next morning Zhang Yu's assistant sent over the short story, the script and a contract. Lu

Dong hadn't slept since he got home at three that morning. He still hadn't said a word to Yiduo. He lay in bed, eyes wide open, not the least bit tired, worrying about all sorts of things. Out of nowhere, he started getting anxious about Zhang Yu's health – what if he died that very day? His daughter wet the bed, and he got up to change the sheets. Lu Fan was eating candy in her dreams, her jaws working away vigorously, her little hands pawing at his face as if to remove a wrapper. The contract was pretty standard, no obvious pitfalls. After he signed it he showed it to Yiduo, then put it in the mail. For some years now, Yiduo has been running a special-effects company which is doing quite well. Mostly she renders adorable demons and scatterbrained gods. She wasn't working that day, so she cooked him lunch and dinner, and in between she read the story and script through carefully. Lu Dong's role is a supporting character who only appears in one of the subplots, and though he has hardly any lines, he's in twenty-three scenes and has a distinctive personality. Most importantly the part suits Lu Dong: his character is a rather dull, emotional person who somehow keeps doing the wrong thing. The story isn't too long, maybe ten thousand words, and the character first appears in the following paragraph:

The gunman lies prone on the ground. Through his scope he can see Old Dong examining the woman's wound, then studying the drawing on the wall. The gunman studies it along with him. It doesn't look finished. According to his understanding of art, it's missing the most important brushstroke. He pulls the trigger. The bullet grazes Old Dong's throat and sinks into the wall. Now the picture's complete. He disassembles the rifle and packs it into his rucksack, rolls up the mat, and leaves. He's Chinese and speaks with a northern accent, but has an English name: Dick.

Dick only works for one man, Boss Chen, whom he met ten years ago while hunting in Africa. In the decade since he's been given three to four jobs a year, each one lasting about two months from preparation to the actual killing. Afterwards, he leaves the country and goes wandering for half a month before coming back. Ever since Dick shot a person for the first time, he's never again hunted an animal.

Back when he was in an acting troupe Lu Dong had fired a real gun, loaded with blanks. He no longer has access to it, and it's illegal to buy even a fake gun online. Which is how, early this morning, Lu Dong comes to be messing around with a clothes-drying pole. In a bid to increase its weight, he wraps a bath towel around it, fastening it in place with a three-finger width of clear tape. All morning he lies prone on his balcony. By May Beijing is already very warm. Lu Dong stares at the T-junction below. To the south of the intersection is a huge shopping mall, built fairly recently, shaped like a ship. The ground floor is all advertisements for well-known brands – the Tesla logo like an inverted anchor sunk into a blood-red backdrop. A narrow road runs to the north, only just wide enough for two lanes of traffic, frequently mired in gridlock. To either side are small shopfronts, from hotpot restaurants to pink-curtained sex shops. This used to be a hutong, and from upstairs he can still see a public restroom tucked away behind the shops. Further along is a petrol station, bulging from the narrow road like an Adam's apple, the main reason it gets so congested here. Lu Dong skips both breakfast and lunch. In the afternoon he lies in bed reading the script. Feeling like his brain is lacking oxygen, he roots around in the fridge and finds an apple, which he eats. That night he's so hungry he can't sleep, and he keeps belching. This contract killer isn't a famine victim, Yiduo says, You can't go on like this. I don't have many lines, so the most important thing is how I look, Lu Dong says. Besides, my face is so greasy, I need to do something about it. Yiduo reaches out to stroke his cheek and says, I understand you, and our daughter does too. Today she told me she's not going to play with you any more, she doesn't want to disturb you. Anyway, you can't just quit eating. Why don't you exercise instead? I'll dig out your running shoes tomorrow. Eat a little less, and start jogging – that's more sustainable.

At six the next morning, while Yiduo is still in bed, Lu Dong makes himself a packet of instant noodles, finds the running shoes himself and goes for a jog around the block. His legs feel so heavy that he doesn't even make it out of his compound, and has to walk back looking like he's been dredged from the water. Now he recalls the last time he exercised: six years ago. This was right after he got married to Yiduo, when they were still living on the west side of the city. He was the breadwinner then. On the weekends they'd head to the university to play badminton, then walk back hand in hand to their tiny apartment. Then Lu Fan was born, and he hasn't exercised since. Yiduo works during the day while Lu Fan is in kindergarten, and normally Lu Dong wouldn't be up this early. Now he heats up milk for the two of them and toasts some bread.

Yiduo eats, but Lu Fan refuses – she wants to have breakfast at kindergarten. Even so, she approves of Lu Dong's new routine. Baba, she says, this way we'll get to spend more time together. Lu Dong now wonders why he used to sleep so much – no particular reason, it's just that he can't drive, so he's not the one who takes his daughter to school. Also, in sleep he feels clean, safe. No matter what troubles you have in your dreams, you can wake up from them, then ah, you're in this empty home, everyone performing their roles, nothing goes wrong, no one sees through him, he lies alone in the soft bed as if he's only just been born. He is afraid of sweet dreams, fears their falseness, fears the moment of waking and realizing he must still endure this happy life, fears understanding that he has committed every conceivable crime but lacks the courage to take responsibility, and that no one even wants him to be held accountable. Before they head out he hugs Yiduo and Lu Fan, lightly grazing his daughter's face with his stubble, feeling both the rightness and the regret within this gesture.

After they leave, Lu Dong eats the rest of the bread, takes up his pole again and resumes his prone position on the balcony. This time round he finds a rug to lean on – actually Lu Fan's bath towel from when she was two, now too small for her, but exactly the right size to cushion his elbows so they stop aching. A tripod would be useful, something to rest the rifle on, but there's nothing like that in the apartment, so he grabs some books from the shelf and places those beneath the barrel.

For the next half hour or so he keeps his eyes fixed on a woman, probably a nanny, leading an enormous black hound on a leash. Its head is the size of a bucket, brown collar as respectable as a necktie, while the woman is scrawny, short-necked and short-limbed, scurrying along ahead of the dog, which keeps stopping. When it extrudes two thick logs of shit, she wraps them in a Kleenex and, looking around to make sure no one's watching, quickly trots over to the ornamental pond in the centre of their compound and flings them in. A boy about Lu Fan's age spots the dog, jumps off his skateboard and insists on clambering onto the dog's back. The dog goes along with it, even half-kneeling to help the boy get on. The boy's mother arrives and scoops him up. The dog licks her ankle, and the mother shrieks. She takes off running with the boy in her arms. Lu Dong aims his rifle at the mother's head, keeping his sights trained on her until she vanishes into another building. When he turns back the dog is gone too, and all he can see is the wind shaking the compound's peach trees, scattering blossoms.

Gazing into the distance, his eyes land on the metro station outside the mall. It's surging with people, the dense crowd like churning slurry. A lone man pushes his way out, one of the very few exiting rather than entering. He crosses the road and goes to the window counter of a grocery store, buys a pack of cigarettes, then heads towards Lu Dong's compound. He is about Lu Dong's age, a little thinner, with a receding hairline that reveals two patches of pale forehead scalp. Light blue jacket and black sweatpants. Lu Dong aims the rifle at him. The man stops outside the compound, rips open the pack and starts to smoke. Seeing him like this through the railings, Lu Dong imagines him as a criminal. What is he here for? Perhaps to steal some rich man's lover. Quite a few mistresses live in this compound, he knows, alone in large apartments. They wear lipstick even if they're just going to the supermarket, sleep all day and all night too. But no, Lu Dong reminds himself, he's meant to be a killer, why would a killer murder a criminal? Outlaws aren't like actors, who readily turn against members of their own profession. Okay, so maybe this guy is a plainclothes police officer who's been tailing Lu Dong for a couple of years now, and has finally tracked him down to where he lives. Take one more step and you're dead, Lu Dong whispers to himself. The man drops his cigarette butt and saunters back the way he came.

A strong wind starts up around noon. The old people resting their legs in the courtyard and the nannies with their young charges all disappear. Bereft of targets, Lu Dong dozes off. When he wakes up, he feels despair – how could a professional killer fall asleep at his post like this? He stands up and gets some cold milk from the fridge, then wanders around the apartment. There are no toy guns anywhere. If only Lu Fan were a boy, he thinks. He texts Yiduo: If it's convenient, could you pick up a toy rifle on your way home? Ideally more than a metre long with a scope. He reads the story again. It's very short and lacks detail. After Boss Chen's death Dick keeps working, and in fact most of the narrative is about this period of his life: after lying low for a while, he begins taking out men who urinate in public. Lu Dong reads the script again, which doesn't provide any more insight into Dick's motivation. Shooting public urinators doesn't earn him any money, and it takes quite a lot of effort. Boss Chen used to tell him the time, place and target, and all he had to do was find a good vantage point, lie in wait, open fire and escape. It's not like he can just wait in the same place with his sights trained on a utility pole, because it would be too easy to find him by following the bullet's trajectory. He'd need to spot an offender, follow him and take him out when he wasn't actually peeing. Maybe he'd be stepping out of a local supermarket or waiting for his kids at the kindergarten gate when the bullet enters his brain from some distant window. Lu Dong texts Zhang Yu:

> *Sir, I'd like to know more about Dick's psychology – who are his parents? Who does he love? Does he prefer tea or Coca-Cola? Does he sleep on his back or his side? After killing someone, does he go for noodles or have a shower? Most importantly, why does he shoot people who urinate in public? Is he a radical environmentalist? Or does he have trouble peeing? Sorry to bother you, any tips you can share would be a great help.*

Zhang Yu doesn't immediately reply.

Lu Dong has a shower, then goes through the script and looks at Dick's lines, all twelve of them:

1. A pack of Esse cigarettes, please. Green, not blue. No, not that one, give me the one third row down, fifth from the left.

2. [*on the phone*] Okay, got it. What kind of lion? Where did it bite you? Please tell your wife I'm broken up about this. I'll never contact you again.

3. See where I'm pointing? Walk down this road. After the first junction, you'll see a Japanese elementary school. Don't turn, keep going straight. At the second junction, there'll be a congee shop on your right. Turn towards it and keep going about five hundred metres to the massage parlour. That's the place you want. The masseur isn't actually blind, he just keeps his eyes shut.

4. I don't like the noodles you made today. I can tell you're in a bad mood – they're all clumping together.

5. This is a you problem, not a me problem. Know the difference. Maybe one day my problems will become your problems, but you should pray that day never comes.

6. People envy birds because they can fly, but I don't. I can shoot them out of the sky anytime I want. I envy the flowing river. You

can't stop a river. Even if you build a
dam, you haven't stopped the river, it's
just waiting.

7. Wrong number.

8. There seems to be a misunderstanding.
I hope that's a business issue, and nothing
personal. If I've accidentally attracted your
attention, that's because you're too sensitive.
People die in this world every single day.
You need to be less sensitive.

9. And another thing, where'd the noodle
shop go?

10. Peeing in public is a dangerous business.
I'm telling you this because you have two
kids. Look up. That thing is called the sun.
It shines down on you and fills each day with
warmth. You shouldn't be living like this.
Build yourself a nice bathroom in your house,
and go enjoy it whenever you feel the urge to
pee. Pass this habit on to your children.

11. Go ahead, study me, put me under the
microscope. Your hearts are dead. What
good could a microscope do you?

12. Could the person who shot me step forward?
Hi, my name's Dick, what's your name?

Lu Dong goes through all these lines, underlining them in pencil, reciting them three times each. Dick's dialogue is odd – a series of non-sequiturs that mostly go unanswered. Not really dialogue at all. Dick doesn't do conversation. Right at the end, the person whose name Dick asks for – an anonymous foot soldier – doesn't even get the chance to step out from his hiding place and speak before Dick dies. Naturally a vigilante who goes around shooting public pissers has to die, but it makes Lu Dong sad to see him end this way. It feels tragic. *Hi, my name's Dick, what's your name?* He reads it twice more, finds the rhythm of the line. No sorrow at his life ending. He just wants to understand this man. *What's your name?* Lu Dong stands before the mirror, staring at his own face. *What's your name?* He makes one corner of his lip twitch up, keeps his eyebrows level, tries to look composed. This is how he'll do it. All of a sudden, he feels he can do the performance justice, or at least this line – his interpretation makes sense, and if someone were to call *action* right now, he's confident everyone would be satisfied with the take.

His phone pings. Zhang Yu:

Just back from swimming. These questions aren't easy to answer. You know me, if I could think clearly

I wouldn't make movies. Forgive me, but actually I'm not sure these questions are important. If you think they are, then please take responsibility for them. I'll give you a tip though: you don't hate your target, but rather you've thought about it rationally and have decided that the world would be a better place if he didn't exist. You're not a foot soldier, because foot soldiers always take the country's side. You're someone who rearranges the world all by yourself, like the great Lei Feng, not bound by ethics, a small-time intellectual. Take care.

Lu Dong responds with a thumbs-up and OK emoji. He thinks he understands.

That evening, Yiduo comes home bearing a toy gun with a scope, though no tripod, and the scope is merely decorative – all he can see through it is grey plastic – while the bullets are plastic orange pellets. You could shoot someone in the face with these and not injure them. In other words, the gun is as harmless as a ping-pong ball dispenser, but at least it has a trigger. A little later, they take Lu Fan out for pizza. She loves western food and can polish off half a nine-inch pizza and a fillet steak all by herself, but she's not fat. It's as if she was born with the ability to transform western food into water and carbon dioxide. Back at home, Lu Dong tells his daughter the story of the Tyrannosaurus rex, a carnivore who falls into a deep gully where there's nothing to eat. A fox falls in love with him and gathers fruit for him each day, and he survives. When the T-Rex finally gets out and returns to the forest he goes back to eating other animals, but whenever he encounters a fox he hesitates and flips a coin to decide if he should eat it. Most of the time, the coin gives him the outcome he desires.

For the next few days, Lu Dong rehearses by himself, taking care of his daughter at night so Yiduo can finish up her work. He wakes up at six each morning to make breakfast for his wife and child. At night, after Lu Fan has gone to bed, he goes downstairs for a jog around the compound in an attempt to reduce the excess flesh on his body and face. Dick only smokes half a pack a day, so Lu Dong does the same. Never any more or any less, ten cigarettes exactly. Now and then he feels a surge of desire for his lover, but the task ahead of him quickly tamps that down. For the first time in five years his feelings are more-or-less pure. A week later, he knows all Dick's lines by heart, he has a plan for the blocking of each scene, and he's come up with a gesture that isn't in the script: before he fires his gun, Dick sticks his right index finger into his ear, then touches that same finger to the trigger. At least two of his meals each day are noodles, sometimes takeout, sometimes home-made. After the first week, he notices a tiny new restaurant by the T-junction that serves Shanxi noodles. Their cleanliness is only so-so but the noodles are tasty, and so he begins going there at lunchtime for a bowl of knife-cut noodles. On the tenth night, he dreams of Dick lurking behind a window in the distance, taking aim at him while he pees by the side of the road. Dick touches his finger to his ear and shoots him dead.

A beautiful nightmare.

On the twenty-third day, as if making a daily visit to church, Lu Dong lies prone on his balcony. The man in the blue jacket appears again at the compound gate. Lu Dong aims the toy gun at his head. A nanny returns from buying groceries and uses her keycard to enter the compound, and the man slips in behind her. Today he is carrying a red rucksack. He walks over to one of the benches by the pond and sits down, gazing around, staring at the koi in the water. It's a sunny day and the pond is glittering. The man sits there quite a while, then seems to remember something, and reaches into his rucksack for a baseball cap, which he puts on, casting a shadow over his face. Lu Dong points the gun at the centre of the cap. The man folds his arms and stares into space. A few residents bring their children to play by the pond. The kids point at the water and seem to say something. One of them sticks a leg in and his mother smacks him. Someone tosses breadcrumbs to the koi, who surge over to snap them up, like petals on a flower. Lu Dong is getting thirsty but stays put. He thinks to himself, if you don't move, neither will I. A half hour passes. A nanny in her forties pushes a stroller up to the pond. In the stroller is a pair of twins, each sleeping in their own little seat. Lu Dong has never seen this nanny or this stroller. Probably the family just moved in, or the babies were born recently. Not talking to anyone, the nanny parks the stroller by the water and settles onto a bench to bask in the sun. Time passes. A boy drops his water pistol into the pond and the wind blows it into the centre. Several parents come over but they aren't able to retrieve it. The nanny stands and seems to be suggesting something. At this moment, the man in the baseball cap quickly walks over to the stroller, places something onto one of the seats, and briskly leaves through the gate.

A bomb? Lu Dong is about to shout down at them but shakes his head. What if it's not a bomb?

What if it's a flyer for an early education centre? Shyness and anxiety do battle in his heart. Finally he gets up, changes into a clean shirt and takes the elevator down. By the time he gets to the lake there is no sign of the nanny or the twins. The little boy's father is scooping up the water pistol with a pool skimmer. Lu Dong looks up at his balcony, where the gun is still propped up and pointing in this direction. He leaves through the gate and makes a round of the perimeter, but there is no sign of the man. Could he have dozed off? Maybe everything he just saw was a dream. At the supermarket, he buys a pack of cigarettes: A pack of Esse cigarettes, please. Green, not blue. No, not that one, give me the one third row down, fifth from the left. The clerk says, What? Lu Dong thinks maybe he didn't hear and repeats the entire line. The clerk says, Sir, we're out of Esse. Look, the shelf's empty. Lu Dong nods and gets some chewing gum instead.

Back home he sits in the study, puts some eye-drops in his eyes, shuts them and has a rest. Time for noodles, he thinks, but he's a little tired, and all of a sudden he misses Lu Fan. If only she could show up now and say she's back early because something happened at the kindergarten. Now he understands that concentration equals loneliness. He opens his eyes and returns to the balcony. The nanny and the twin stroller are back by the pond. He senses the *tick tick* of a timer. He ought to have eliminated that man earlier, he realizes. What a slip-up. This could be a micro-bomb, no thicker than a human hair. Or something even more advanced, a see-through bomb. You'd never spot that before it exploded, yet it might be powerful enough to decimate an entire building. He should have known from the first moment he set eyes on the man that he was the sort who brings wickedness into the world. Lu Dong was the only one who noticed, and now he's let him get away.

He checks the time on his phone and sees a text from Zhang Yu's production manager:

Director Zhang Yu drowned while swimming at three o'clock this afternoon. The film has been cancelled, and your contract is now invalid. More details to follow. We are all shocked and saddened. Legal proceedings against the swimming pool have begun. Our condolences. Be well.

It's six o'clock. Lu Dong calls Yiduo but she doesn't pick up. Then he remembers she's taken Lu Fan to her piano lesson and is having dinner with some of the other parents. His heart judders like an airplane plummeting, plummeting, still not reaching the ground. He thinks to himself, This is a you problem, not a me problem. Know the difference. Maybe one day my problems will become your problems, but you should pray that day never comes. And another problem: the timer in his head is still going *tick tick*, not pausing for a second. He steps out onto the balcony. The sun is beginning to set, and there are more people gathering downstairs – children, adults, dogs, people with kites, skateboards, water pistols shaped like animal heads. He sees the nanny sitting next to the twin stroller, one leg hoisted onto the other, snacking on melon seeds from her hand-kerchief. The man in the baseball cap is on a nearby bench, still wearing his red rucksack, hands clasped, head lowered. Lu Dong goes into the kitchen and gets a knife, a couple of handspans long with a sharp point. He wraps this in newspaper, tucks it under his arm and gets the elevator down. By the time he's reached the pond the man is nowhere to be seen. Whirling around, he spots the man walking out of the compound gate. Lu Dong swats the handker-chief out of the nanny's hand and says, There's something in your stroller, get the kids out quick. With that he chases after the man, but there's no sign of him. He remembers that he first saw him approach from the T-junction and heads that way, pausing a few seconds when he reaches the noodle shop, or rather where the noodle shop used to be – it's gone now, in its place a roller shutter with a microscope painted on it.

Lu Dong sprints through the crowds surging up from the subway station and catches up with the man in the middle of the intersection. He knocks him to the ground. Lu Dong puts the point of the knife to his throat and says, What did you put in the stroller?

– What stroller?

– The twins' stroller. And another thing, where did the noodle shop go?

– What noodle shop?

– There used to be one on the street back there, where'd it go?

– Oh, you mean the Shanxi noodle place. I've been wondering that too.

Lu Dong sticks a finger into his ear with his free hand, allowing the knife point to skate across the man's throat.

– Don't change the subject. What did you put in the stroller?

– A rag doll.

– What's inside it?

– Rags, obviously.

An Audi speeds by, honking loudly.

– Why did you put the rag doll in there?

– I miss my children. That's why I did it. I have two daughters, but I know something's wrong with me, something unforgivable, and I'll never see them again. Go ahead and stab me dead, solve all my problems, though you'll only be creating problems for yourself.

Lu Dong abruptly feels air swirling up from his chest, leaving through his mouth, his nose, his ears, while at the same time his flesh creeps downwards. A weightless distant spirit takes hold of his legs, and he can't stop himself from falling over. He drops the knife and sits beside the man amid the flowing traffic, and he looks up into the distance, where perhaps someone is taking aim at him, judgement for all the wrongs he's done since he was born. But so what? The man pats him on the shoulder and says, You take life too seriously, don't you? Lu Dong says nothing. He can see a river not far away, rippling beneath the thronging twilit crowds, completely clear, fish darting through it, the water lush with aquatic plants, no thought of sluice gates, no fear of bullets, flowing all the way to the vast ocean.

Quoted Matter

p. 19   *'Still young, still idealistic . . . He has no idea what to do.'* : from 'Father' (父亲) by Zhang Zao (张枣).

p. 68   'For ten years now the living and dead have been parted': from Su Dongpo's elegy to his wife, who had been dead for a decade (江城子·乙卯正月二十日夜记梦).

p. 164 *'The business intrusted to this fellow . . . it did not appear clear to me what he was waiting for*: from *Heart of Darkness* by Joseph Conrad.

p. 174 'when things grow too long they turn into snakes': from Giovanni Verga's 1888 novel *I Malavoglia*, translated as *The House by the Medlar-Tree* by Mary A. Craig (1890).

p. 179 'A Letter always feels to me like immortality because it is the mind alone without corporeal friend.': letter from Emily Dickinson to Thomas Wentworth Higginson, June 1869.